# Filthy Wicked

# LOVE

## Kidnapped by the Billionaire
## Book One

### By Lili Valente

Contains the series starter
Dirty Twisted Love and the
full-length novel Filthy Wicked Love

# *Filthy Wicked* LOVE

By Lili Valente

Self Taught Ninja Press

Copyright © 2016 Lili Valente
All rights reserved
ISBN 13: 978-1533347213

## All Rights Reserved

Copyright **Filthy Wicked Love** © 2016 Lili Valente

All rights reserved. Without limiting the rights under copyright reserved above, no part of this publication may be reproduced, stored in or introduced into a retrieval system, or transmitted, in any form, or by any means (electronic, mechanical, photocopying, recording, or otherwise) without the prior written permission of the copyright owner. This erotic romance is a work of fiction. Names, characters, places, brands, media, and incidents are either the product of the author's imagination or are used fictitiously. The author acknowledges the trademarked status and trademark owners of various products referenced in this work of fiction, which have been used without permission. The publication/use of these trademarks is not authorized, associated with, or sponsored by the trademark owners. This book is licensed for your personal use only. This book may not be re-sold or given away to other people. If you would like to share this book with another person, please purchase an additional copy for each person you share it with, especially if you enjoy hot, sexy, emotional novels featuring Dominant alpha males. If you are reading this book and did not purchase it, or it was not purchased for your use only, then you should return it and purchase your own copy. Thank you for respecting the author's work. Cover design by Bootstrap Designs. Editorial services provided by Leone Editorial.

# About the Book

**Warning: This book is rough and raw, dark and delicious, and hot enough to set your panties on fire. Read with caution (and spare panties).**

The first time billionaire turned CIA agent Clay Hart fell for Harley Mason, she nearly killed him. But she won't get another chance at his heart or his life. He's going to take the son she's hidden from him for years, send her to jail where she belongs, and never look back.

Harley isn't the sick twisted person she used to be, but sins have a long half-life and rage an even longer reach. Now the only man she's ever loved is back from the dead and determined to take away her reason for living. But she won't give up her son without one hell of a dirty, twisted, sexy fight.

She won't give up.

He won't give in.

And neither of them is prepared for the sparks that fly between them or the shared enemy determined to destroy them both.

Harley and Clay are each determined to win the filthy, wicked game they play. But sometimes even the sexiest games turn deadly, leaving innocent lives caught in the crossfire…

Dedicated to my Wicked Review Crew
Much love for all you do!

# DIRTY TWISTED LOVE

Kidnapped by the Billionaire 0.5

(This prequel should be read before Filthy Wicked Love)

By Lili Valente

# CHAPTER ONE

Harley

*J*ust a few more weeks.

Just a few more weeks, one last job, and she and Jasper would finally be safe.

Harley studied her reflection in the small mirror above the outdoor sink, trying to see if she was buying her own encouraging load of bullshit. But her blue eyes were cool and calm. Her eyes kept their secrets, refusing to say if they believed in happily ever after.

*Happily ever after. Riiiight.*

*I'm sure that's right around the corner, along with Santa Claus and Prince Charming riding a unicorn.*

She turned to face the beach with a sigh the sea breeze swept away. Happily ever after was definitely a long shot. At this point, she would settle for being able to stop looking over her shoulder and take for granted that she would live to see her thirtieth birthday. Ian Hawke—her father's enemy and the man who had nearly killed Harley and her twin sister, Hannah, last December—was dead, but her own enemies were still very much among the living.

Marlowe Reynolds considered her a friend, or at least a trusted associate, but if he realized she wanted out, she would see the terrifying side of the soft-spoken Brit. He was the most successful drug lord in Europe, and a man didn't run a multi-billion dollar cartel for over a decade without knowing how to keep his friends close, his enemies dead, and people who knew too much tucked firmly beneath his wing. Marlowe didn't let people walk away;

he made the malcontent disappear. In order to make her escape, Harley was going to have to be very smart, very careful, and very lucky.

Smart and careful she could control, but luck didn't take directions.

Therefore, precautions had to be taken.

Harley's gaze drifted to the sheltered section of the private beach, where Jasper was busy digging a hole so deep only the top of his tousled blond hair showed above the sand. Before she and Dominic had started running sprints along the shoreline, she'd asked Jasper what he was digging for, but he'd refused to say, only giving her a mysterious grin and a vague "you'll see."

With his dark blond hair, murky blue eyes several shades darker than her own, and golden skin, Jasper looked like his father, but he kept his secrets close to his chest like his mother.

Sometimes Harley worried that he was too much like her, and that his insatiable curiosity would lead him into the same labyrinth she'd wandered most of her life, a place where the walls of perception were always shifting and each ugly new revelation only forced you deeper into the maze. But most of the time she believed in nurture triumphing over nature. She wasn't raising Jasper the way she had been raised. He was being taught that kindness was a strength, not a signal to attack at will, and as he grew she would continue to help him channel his curiosity into more productive pursuits than the ones she'd been steered toward.

Engineering, maybe. Jasper loved building things, even though he claimed he was going to be a "destruction worker" when he grew up.

"Is that smile for me?" Dominic asked, his dark eyes flashing as he walked up the trail from the beach.

Harley tilted her head to one side, letting her grin stretch wider. "It could be. If you say the torture is over for the day."

"Not yet, beautiful." Dominic's hand lingered on her waist. He nodded toward the makeshift weight room he'd set up on the covered patio. "Come on, let's do legs and abs and then we'll call it a day."

Her sister Hannah's former bodyguard had spent the past three months whipping Harley into the best physical shape of her life, insisting she needed to keep her body as sharp as her mind. In addition to serving as her personal trainer, he was also concealing her whereabouts from her sister's psychotic new husband, Jackson, a man Harley suspected wanted to kill her. Not that Jackson didn't have every reason to want her dead after what she'd done to him, but she had a son to raise. She had to stay alive and Dom was helping make that happen.

In exchange, Harley spent several hours a day sweating in the brutal Thai sun and her nights pretending she didn't realize that her lover would rather be sleeping with her sister.

"Let me get Jasper into the bath," she said, catching Dom's hand and giving it a light squeeze. "I'll meet you there."

"All right." He stretched his arms overhead, his white tee shirt riding up high enough to reveal the taut planes of his stomach. "I already put his boogie board away. All he needs to do is grab his sand toys."

"Thanks," she murmured, letting her eyes skim up and down Dom's frame. He was a beautiful man—long and lean, with muscles on top of muscles, caramel skin, amber-flecked eyes, and a classically handsome face. It had certainly been no hardship to spend a few months on a beach with him, but it wouldn't hurt to say goodbye. She had enjoyed their time together, but she wasn't looking for long-term attachments.

She only had space in her heart for Jasper. Her son was her first—and only—priority. There wasn't room in her crazy life for anything else.

"But don't be too long," Dom continued, backing away. "We should leave by four. Traffic's been bad getting in and out of town since the mudslide."

Harley nodded and started across the sand to help Jasper gather up his toys. He loved bath time and would play until his skin was pruned all over if she let him. Today she would set his timer for an hour. That should give her plenty of time to finish her workout, grab a quick shower, and finish packing Jasper's bag for the trip. Maybe his last trip.

*Please let it be the last.*

She didn't know how much longer she could keep sending her son away not knowing when or if she would ever see him again.

"Tub time," she said, forcing a smile as she squatted down at the edge of Jasper's sand pit. "Have you found the buried treasure yet?"

"I'm not finding it, I'm leaving it." Jasper scrambled out and began tossing his extensive collection of sand toys, favorite red shovel, and alligator beach towel down inside the hole. "I've already drawn a map to leave in my room. That way the next kid who lives here can go on a hunt for my treasure and then we'll be friends."

Harley's throat tightened. "So I guess you saw your suitcase in the laundry room."

"You can't take sand toys on the airplane," Jasper said, not meeting her eyes as he shoved a mound of sand toward the edge of the pit, sending it sliding down on top of his treasures. "A little help here, lady?"

"I'm not a lady, I'm your mother," she said,

finishing her part of their inside joke even though her heart wasn't in it. But neither was Jasper's, and he wasn't moping. He was burying treasures for a friend he would never meet.

She helped him fill in the hole, not bothering to tell him that the tide would probably wash away his treasures long before any other child came to find them. She'd chosen this island off the coast of Thailand because it was remote, sparsely populated, and far outside the stomping grounds of the typical tourist. The rental house they'd leased had stood empty for a year before they had come to stay and would probably stay empty for months after she had packed up their things.

After the sand was smooth again, she and Jasper stomped over the top a few times, tamping it down until a darker, damper spot than the surrounding sand was the only sign that the beach had been disturbed.

With one last stomp, Jasper took her hand. "Are you coming this time, Mama?"

"No," Harley said, leading the way back

toward the bungalow. "Dominic is going to be your travel buddy. I have to take care of a few things and close up the house. Then I'll come meet you. It shouldn't be more than two weeks, three at the most."

Jasper frowned. "What about Miss Louisa? Am I still supposed to call her if something goes wrong?"

"Yes. Call Miss Louisa first and if she's not available call Mr. Tim and he'll know what to do." Harley hated that her six-year-old was so intimately acquainted with potential danger, but their plans and backup plans had kept Jasper safe when she was taken captive last December. If some of his innocence had to die in order to keep him alive, it was a price she was willing to pay. "But you know Dom is smart and careful. You shouldn't have any problems and you'll be having so much fun exploring a new city you won't even have a chance to miss me."

Jasper dropped her hand to turn on the waterspout near the door and leaned down to rinse his arms and legs. "I would rather stay at the beach with you. I like the beach better than the city. Even Paris."

"Me, too," she said, ruffling his sandy hair. "Maybe someday soon we'll have a forever house on the beach."

*Or you will, when I'm dead and you go to live with Hannah on her island.*

Harley pushed the thought away and helped Jasper get the sand out from between his toes. She wasn't going to die and leave Jasper to be raised by someone else. Hannah would love him like her own, Harley was sure of it, but Hannah's husband, Jackson, was another matter.

Harley had done terrible, unforgivable things to Jackson back when she was a young woman with more lust for vengeance than sense. Framing a man for rape had been one of her uglier moments, but whether Jackson's hatred for her was justified or not, she didn't want her son raised by a man who might make Jasper pay for her sins.

Jasper had never known anything but a mother who loved him more than life and that's how things were going to stay. He was never going to know what it felt like to be shut out of a parental figure's heart.

"Can I bring my bath toys on the plane?" Jasper asked as they let themselves into the house and headed for the bathroom.

"We can buy more bath toys at our new place." Harley started the water running, making sure it was a little on the hot side since Jasper would be playing for a while, and turned to help him undress. "But I have a special surprise for you. I'll give it to you at the airport."

Jasper's head popped free of his blue rash guard, his eyes dancing. "Is it for my collection?"

Harley shrugged mysteriously. "You'll have to wait and see." She leaned in, cupping his chubby cheeks and pressing a kiss to his sun-warmed forehead. "Remember to turn the water off before it gets too full, okay? And scrub your hair good. You don't want to carry sand with you onto the plane."

"I don't care." Jasper shoved his trunks down, sending the sand in his swimsuit spilling out all over the tile. "I like sand."

"Obviously," Harley said dryly, watching

him climb into the tub, her heart breaking a little bit.

He was so beautiful, so sweet, and so much like his father there was no way she would ever be able to forget the man she'd lost too soon, before she'd realized that punishing the people who'd wronged her would never fill the empty place in her soul.

But that was all right. She didn't want to forget Clay and she never wanted to take her son—or the way he'd changed her—for granted. Jasper had saved her life, pure and simple. He was her everything and she would do whatever it took to keep him safe.

Even if it meant one last dance with the devil in the pale moonlight.

Marlowe was a bad man, but Harley was no angel, and sometimes one thing must die for another to be born from the ashes.

With one last look at Jasper—doing her best to memorize the blissed-out expression on his face as he dumped his bath toys out of their bucket into the water—she closed the bathroom door and went to set the first stage of her plan into motion.

## CHAPTER TWO

Harley

"We're not skipping legs and abs." Dominic shook his head, pointing to the mat he'd spread out on the patio. "Give me a plank hold. Let's see if you can break yesterday's record."

Harley crossed her arms and stood her ground. "No. Exercise interferes with my focus and we need to talk. There's not much time left."

Dom's full lips curved at the edges. "We could have talked for hours last night after Jasper went to bed. You're shameless, H. Any excuse to get out of a workout."

"There's a reason I was happily scrawny and lacking in muscle tone before you came into my life." She let him draw her into his arms and linked her wrists behind his neck, running her fingers through his silky black hair. "I need the contact information for your friends in Bangkok. I think I've figured out a way to get free from Marlowe, but I'm going to need help."

Dom's grin faded. "The people I know in Bangkok aren't nice people, Harley."

"I don't need nice people. I need people who won't have a problem breaking into the house while I'm asleep, roughing me up, and leaving enough of a mess behind that anyone who bothers to look will assume I didn't make it out alive."

"A mess?" His brows drew together. "What kind of mess?"

"Blood, probably some tissue too," she said frankly. There was no time for either one of them to be squeamish. That's why she'd waited to bring this up. She didn't want him to be able to put her off. She wanted him under the gun with no choice but to give her the names she needed. "And it has to be mine. Marlowe will have it tested. He doesn't leave boxes unchecked."

Dom tried to pull away, but she held tight to his neck. "It'll be okay. I've lost a lot of blood before and been just fine."

"Yeah, I was there," he snapped, wrapping his fingers around her wrists, breaking her grip, and holding her hands captive between them. "You weren't fine. You almost died. If your dad hadn't had a doctor on call, you might have."

"The only way Marlowe is going to let me go is if he thinks I'm dead," she insisted. "You know I'm right."

"I do. That's why you need me here to help you." He gentled his touch. "Let's cancel the flight today. We can call your friend Louisa, put Jasper on a plane to Paris as an unaccompanied minor, and—"

"No." She pulled her hands free with a shake of her head. "Jasper can't go back to Paris. Ian's men found me there. That means Marlowe's could follow the trail, too. They would figure out who my friends are and they would eventually find Jasper. I can't risk that. Marlowe can never know about Jasper."

"You think he doesn't know already?" Dom said, pacing toward the rack of free weights at the edge of the patio. "He's fucking paranoid as hell, Harley. I'm sure he knows everything about you, right down to what color you shit in the morning."

Her nose wrinkled, but she refused to dignify that comment with a response.

"You need me here with you," Dom continued, prowling back toward her. "If someone is going to help you fake your death it should be me. At least you know I won't sell you as a sex slave while you're unconscious."

"I'm too old for the slave trade," she said, a part of her wishing Dom was still on her father's payroll so she could get away with giving him orders and expecting them to be obeyed. "They like innocent little girls, not twenty-nine-year-old mothers."

His lips parted, but she cut him off before he could speak.

"And I'm not going to change my mind about this. I need you with Jasper. If you really want to do what's best for me, then take care of him." She closed the distance between them, taking his hand in both of hers. "Please, Dom. You're the only one I trust to be prepared for whatever happens. Louisa is wonderful, but she doesn't know how to handle a gun or how to find Hannah if things don't go as planned."

His eyes narrowed "You can't be serious."

"I don't have anyone else," she said. "I won't let Jasper be raised by my parents, and Aunt Sybil isn't in good enough health to raise a child. Hannah is the only one I trust to love him the way he deserves to be loved."

"She's married to a psychopath," Dom said. "That's the only reason I agreed to keep your location a secret in the first place, Harley. To keep you and Jasper safe from him. Jackson loves Hannah now, but I saw the way he treated her in the beginning. He's a monster. I would never trust him with a child."

"So I guess I'll just have to do my best not to die," she said with a soft laugh.

His scowl deepened. "That isn't funny. None of this is funny. You should never have gotten involved with a man like Marlowe."

"I know that now, Dom," she said, checking her impatience. "But when I met him I was a single mom who couldn't risk coming out of hiding, wondering how I was going to make ends meet when Daddy's money ran out."

"Stewart would have given you more."

"I didn't want more," she snapped. "All I want from Stewart is for him to be out of my and Jasper's lives. Permanently. This is the only way to do that. I finish the job, collect my last paycheck, and disappear in a way that ensures Marlowe doesn't come looking for me."

Dom sighed. It was a put-upon sound, but she could tell she was winning. She just needed to drive her argument home.

"And then Jasper and I can find a house in a little village in a corner of the world where Marlowe and my father and all the other bad guys will leave us alone and we'll be out of your hair for good." She leaned into him with a smile. "And then all you'll need to worry about is how you're going to spend the twenty grand I'm going to pay you for services rendered."

"I don't want your money." His arm went around her waist, holding her close. "And maybe I don't want you out of my hair, either."

Harley looked up at him, chest tightening at the soft look in his eyes. "You don't mean that. I'm not the one you want, Dom. We both know that."

"Don't tell me what I want." He bent low, silencing her with a kiss. His tongue slipped between her lips and his hand plunged into her hair, drawing her closer. He kissed her with a hunger she hadn't felt from him before, but she knew this was as much about being forced to say goodbye as anything he might feel for her.

It was easy to mistake the thing that was hard to get for the thing you really wanted. She'd been swept away by her share of unattainable men when she was younger, before she'd met the man who had taught her that love was sweetest when you didn't have to fight for it. Loving Clay had come easily. Being with him was the most natural thing in the world, like breathing, like she'd been born to laugh at his jokes, fit perfectly in his arms, and get lost making love in a way she never had before.

She hadn't made love to anyone else—before or since. The part of her that had been capable of that kind of closeness had died in the car crash with Clay.

Even as her body came to life, responding to Dom's kiss and the feel of his hand up her shirt, under her bra, rolling her nipple between his fingers, her heart remained calm and quiet. She let Dom pick her up and carry her into the bedroom, locking the door behind them before laying her on the bed, because he needed this and she needed him. She needed his help and she needed to feel something good before he and Jasper left and took all the light in her world with them.

She was a strong woman and she pretended to be even stronger, but there were times when she needed softness in her life.

She needed Dom's mouth hot on her bare skin and his tongue flicking across her nipple before he suckled her hard enough to bow her back off the bed. She needed his rough palms smoothing over her hips to grip her behind the knees and spread her wide, needed his thick fingers fucking her slow and deep while their tongues fought a battle they were both going to win. She needed his cock at her entrance, pushing inside, filling her, building the sweet tension swelling low in her body.

But she didn't love him.

When he stared deep into her eyes as he began to move, silently asking her to let him in, she closed her eyes and buried her face in his neck. Her hands trailed down to claw into the thick muscles of his ass. She urged him to thrust faster, harder, to take them both where they needed to go, but she didn't give him any reason to believe that this was more than a moment of shared pleasure.

This wasn't the beginning or the end or anything worth writing home about. It was a moment to catch their breath and brace themselves for the downpour before running back out into the rain.

"Damn, Harley," Dom whispered against her forehead. "You feel so good. Look at me, baby. Look at me. Let me see you."

Harley relaxed back onto the pillow with a moan and gave the man what he was asking for. She held his gaze as she lifted into his thrusts, letting him see her face twist as she neared the edge, letting him watch as her orgasm claimed her, rippling through her body with enough force to make her lips part in a soundless scream.

But most importantly, she let him see the emptiness at her core, the calm, untouchable pool where the water never rippled and no man would ever see his reflection. It was a lifeless place, ruled by the ghost of a dead man and no other man would ever stake his claim on it.

There were other worlds inside of her,

where friends were treasured, where Hannah was loved with a ferocity only twins could understand, and where Jasper had ruled as the prince of her heart since the moment he looked up at her and blinked his eyes for the first time. But there was no place for what Dom wanted.

It was as impossible as asking the sun to rise in the west or the stars to shine through the daylight.

"Fine," Dom said, hurt flashing in his eyes as his jaw clenched tight. "I get it, but you're going to come for me again. If this is the last time I fuck you, I want to be sure you remember it."

Without another word, he pulled out and flipped her over on her belly. A moment later, he drove into her from behind. Harley groaned as she gave in to him, letting him take her hard and rough if that's what he needed. She would come for him again—he was an amazing lover, that had never been the problem—and he would be able to get off without looking into her cold, dead eyes.

Now that she had dyed her hair back to its

natural brown and grown it as long as her sister's, maybe he would be able to pretend he was fucking Hannah. The good sister, the one he really wanted, the one everyone loved.

And why shouldn't they—Hannah had been born whole and sweet of spirit without any inclination to self-destruct and take the world out with her. Hannah was easy to love. Harley was complicated and hard to handle and sharp to the touch, even when she was trying her best not to hurt anyone.

"I should have known. You never said my name while we were in bed," Dom said, his breath harsh as he reached beneath her, fingers finding her clit. "Never, not one single time."

"Dom, please," she said, but he cut her off before she could finish.

"Don't say it now, it's too late. I just want you to come," he said, riding her harder as his finger circled the top of her sex, making her gasp as she neared the edge a second time. "Come and then I'll come and I'll leave and take care of Jasper, just like you want me to."

She wanted to thank him, but she knew he

wouldn't appreciate it, so she didn't say a word. She just let her head fall back and her hips tilt as she came a second time, her channel contracting so tight it would have forced Dom from her body if he hadn't tightened his grip on her hips, keeping them fused together as his cock jerked inside of her.

She came in long, fierce waves, but the pleasure was bittersweet.

Because Dom was right. This was the last time. They had stopped at different places on the road and now the bridge had washed away, leaving them no way forward or back, at least not together.

"It wasn't her," he murmured, his lips kissing her sweat-slicked shoulder as he spoke. "I know you think it was, but the only person on my mind, when we were like this, was you. I could have loved you if you'd let me. I already love Jasper. So maybe think about him the next time you're ready to get rid of someone who cares about you. You may not want more than this, but there's no reason to shut love out of Jasper's life."

He pulled away, leaving her on her belly on

the bed as he disappeared into the master bathroom to dispose of the condom. Harley heard the shower start and rolled over, staring up at the fan whirring softly above her.

Her throat went tight and the backs of her eyes began to sting, but before the tears could fall, a brisk wind from deep inside of her swirled to the surface, freezing the surge of emotion. Soon her inner world was cold and still once more.

It was the way things were. She couldn't change it, even if she tried.

Dom was wrong. It wasn't that she didn't *want* more than this. She wasn't capable of more than this. He was asking her to spread her arms and fly, stubbornly refusing to see that her wings had been ripped off a long time ago, the day she'd lost the only man she would ever love.

# CHAPTER THREE

Harley

They were quiet on the way to the airfield on the other side of Ko Tao. Harley sat in the backseat of the tiny Figaro she'd bought their first week here, letting Dom play chauffeur as she cuddled Jasper. She did her best to memorize the feel of her son's firm, warm body fitted against hers and the way the setting sun turned his drying curls into a golden halo around his head. She tried not to think about Dom and Jasper flying away, leaving her alone to take care of her unfinished business.

She had the names of Dom's contacts in Bangkok, enough clay and other materials to make sure the statues with Marlowe's drugs hidden inside were ready to ship by Friday, and an exit strategy.

This was going to work. It *had* to work. It was past time to stop running and give Jasper the forever home they'd both been dreaming about for so long.

"Update the blog when you get there so I know you've landed safely," Harley said, avoiding eye contact with Dom as he fetched his and Jasper's suitcases from the trunk. "Don't call or text. We don't want any traceable communication."

"I know." Dom sounded more tired than annoyed. But Harley had been told she was exhausting more times than she could count, so she wasn't really surprised. "And I'll post something every few days so you know we're still doing fine."

"Thank you." Harley put her arm around Jasper. He leaned heavily against her, clearly worn out after his long, last day on the beach. "I appreciate what you're doing for us, Dom."

"Of course." His smile was stiff until he transferred his gaze to Jasper and his expression warmed. "We're going to have fun, aren't we, buddy? We'll play video games the whole way there."

Jasper pumped his fist in the air. "Yes! No reading!"

"Do *some* reading," Harley said, tapping her fingers on top of Jasper's head. "You need to keep that big beautiful brain of yours growing."

"What about Dom's brain?" Jasper asked.

"My brain's done growing," Dom said wryly. "But I'll read some, too. Keep you company."

"Okay." Jasper turned expectantly to Harley. "So I guess all that's left is my surprise."

"I guess so." She grinned as she reached into the open trunk, pulling out a paper bag that she handed over to Jasper. This was the only good part of saying goodbye, seeing the look on his face as he revealed the latest addition to his collection of keeper toys, the playthings that went with them no matter where they moved.

He tore into the bag, giggling with delight as he pulled out the hideous doll she'd ordered online. It was half plastic and half fur, with the head of a Sasquatch, the body of a kewpie doll, and a red and gold skirt with green snakes printed on it. "Oh, Mom, it's so ugly. Maybe the ugliest one yet!"

"I know," Harley said, laughing with him. "I had to search a long time for something uglier than the teddy bear with the chicken pox, but this guy…" She shook her head, her upper lip curling. "He's something else."

"You two are weirdos," Dom said, the affection in his voice making her glance up to find him smiling at Jasper. "Why an ugly toy collection?"

"Because ugly toys are awesome and need homes, too." Jasper clutched the monstrosity to his chest with one arm while he hugged Harley with the other. "Thanks, Mom. I love it."

"You're welcome." She leaned over, pressing a kiss to the top of his head, spotting the grains of sand still clinging to his scalp because, of course, he hadn't bothered to take her scrubbing suggestion seriously.

She didn't know why, but the sight of that sand made her even sadder to see him go. She had to fight to keep from crying as she walked Dom and Jasper to the airfield gate to meet the charter pilot she'd hired to take them to Bangkok and then on to Prague, where they would spend the rest of June.

"It's going to be okay," Dom said, resting a hand on her back, the compassion in his touch making her hope they might find their way back to being friends again, someday. "We'll be fine and we'll see you in a few weeks. Be careful."

She nodded, swallowing hard. "I will. You, too."

"Goodbye, Mom." Jasper hugged her again, clinging tightly. "Never ever."

Her eyes squeezed closed. It was what she'd always said to Hannah. It meant more than I love you. It meant you never ever wanted to be without the other person.

"Never ever, bug," she said, hugging him hard, silently promising him that she would do everything she could to make sure he never had to be without anyone he loved. "Have fun and I'll see you soon."

She stood by the chain link fence, watching Dom and Jasper cross the hard packed dirt to where the small charter plane was waiting, concentrating on the warm wind stirring her hair and the gentle kiss of the evening sun on her skin.

It was time to ground herself in her body, in the moment, and let go of everything that didn't serve her. She needed to be sharp, focused, and ready to respond to danger at a moment's notice. Missing Jasper, worrying about what might happen to her son while she wasn't there to protect him, and stressing about all the things that could go wrong in the next few days would only make her scattered and weak.

If she was going to pull this off, there was no room for weakness. It was time to become the woman she had been before Clay, before Jasper, before the years had taught her how hard it was to lose the things that made life worth living. Now wasn't the time for grief or regret. It was time for hard, sharp, and ruthless.

By the time the plane took off, swinging out over the water before turning north toward the city, Harley's pulse had slowed and emotion no longer fisted in her chest. She turned away from the fence, walking back to the car, focusing on lengthening and smoothing her breath and letting go of thought. It was a trick she'd learned from the man who had taught her how to fly a plane, a former Soviet spy turned smuggler for Marlowe. Quieting the inner world left more resources available to observe the outer world, and depriving the ego of fuel allowed instinct to take over.

Instinct, which only cared about one thing—survival at any cost.

Slowly, Harley's awareness expanded to take in the light glinting off the ocean waves, the murmurs from the wild chickens pecking in the ditch, and the competing scents of ocean and airplane fuel on the wind. Her body slipped into ancient predator-prey mode, scanning her surroundings for cues that would tell her when to fight and when to flee.

If she hadn't shifted her awareness, she might not have noticed the battered red truck on the other side of the field, parked down by the beach just before the black rocks turned to sand. She might not have seen the fisherman leaning over his tackle box and certainly wouldn't have noticed the sandy hair sticking out from beneath his stained ball cap.

She hadn't made any friends on the island—she deliberately kept to herself—but she recognized most of the locals she ran into around town and none of the ex-pats or Brits she'd met were men with blond hair. She supposed the man could be one of the more adventurous backpackers, come to explore the coral reef on the other side of the island, but the few tourists who came to Ko Tao rented scooters to get around. They didn't drive trucks or dress in weathered Thai fisherman's pants.

There was something off about the man who kept his back turned to her as she paused, the car door in hand, studying him over the top of her sun-warmed hood. After a long beat, she slid into the driver's seat and adjusted the mirror until she captured the man's reflection. She started the car, watching him with her foot on the brake, but he didn't turn around. He was focused on the line in his hands, and his face was invisible in the deep shadow beneath the brim of his hat.

Finally, Harley shifted into drive and pulled out onto the road. But when she came to the corner where she would usually turn left to make her way back to the house, she turned right, heading toward town. She'd hit the market yesterday to get everything she needed for the week, but her gut told her not to go home right away. She would feel better being surrounded by other people, at least for a little while.

When she reached the village, she parked just past the gas station and circled around to the trunk. She grabbed her straw hat and settled it on her head, taking her time fetching her cloth bags and shaking the sand from the fabric. As she moved, she scanned the road and the people milling about the open air market near the temple, but the early evening village scene was fairly typical.

There were a few stray dogs fighting over some rotted fruit near the curb, two teen boys without shirts on tinkering with a moped motor, their ribs showing through their nut brown skin, and a group of older women laughing over something on the shortest woman's cell phone as they leaned against the side of the temple. The contrast of the traditional Malay clothing, the dusty street that hadn't changed significantly in the past century, and the iPhone in a case with bright pink cherry blossoms jarred her the way things like that still did, even after months on the island. But aside from that brief flicker of "not right" nothing in the scene pinged her radar.

Slamming the trunk closed, she moved down the side of the road toward the market. There were no sidewalks here, but considering almost everyone drove mopeds or bicycles it wasn't really an issue. There was plenty of room for people and vehicles on the road, as well as the occasional pickup trundling along with a bed full of local men bound for some construction project.

She wouldn't have bought a car except that she had needed to transport large amounts of clay for her sculptures from the post office in town to her house and she didn't want Jasper clinging to her waist as she zipped around on a moped the way the locals with kids did. There weren't any other Caucasian children on the island—the non-local population was composed of older people who had retired here, scientists studying the turtle population, and a few musty-looking men Harley suspected were growing weed in the forest.

Jasper, with his blond curls, would have attracted attention and been remembered—two things Harley had always been careful about, especially since moving to the island.

In Paris, it had been easier to blend in and hide in plain sight. But then she'd made the mistake of getting too settled in, of making friends and establishing patterns that could be observed and predicted. Ian Hawke's men had caught up with her near the flower market, where she'd gone every Wednesday to get fresh flowers for the flat. Even as she'd fought them, struggling to free herself and get back to Jasper, she'd cursed herself for making herself an easy target.

With that in mind, she veered across the street, stopping into the café for a Thai iced coffee, something she hadn't done in months.

She perched on a stool overlooking the street and watched the world go by. There was a steady stream of mopeds headed inland from the ocean, several bicycles, and a four-wheeler with two skinny, barefoot children sharing the perch behind their father, but no larger vehicles and nothing suspicious. She stayed to see which of the dogs won the battle for the squashed mango—the little one with only one ear, never underestimate the underdog—and then slid to the ground and back out onto the street.

At the market, she took the opposite of her usual route, hitting the fish market first and buying a snapper filet, then stopping by the vegetable stalls for eggplant and cilantro before ending at the spice monger, who also sold cans of coconut milk she would need for fish soup. Once her purchases were snug in her bags, she took the long route back to the main road, circling around the back of the temple as the sun set, keeping her senses on high alert.

But she arrived back at the car without seeing or sensing anything strange. She scanned the road one last time, finding it even quieter than when she'd arrived an hour ago, before sliding into the car and heading for home. The island was beautiful at dusk and the smell of salt water and night flowers opening in the cooler air soothed the stress of navigating the winding pass through the mountain and back down toward the coast.

She passed a few people headed into town, but by the time she reached the dirt road leading to the cottage, the road had been abandoned for miles. Once she shut off the car, there wasn't a sound aside from the waves rubbing gently against the shore and birds chattering in the palm trees as she passed beneath them.

An hour later, Harley had spicy coconut fish soup simmering on the stove, a beer in hand, and was sitting on the patio, trying not to think about how weirdly quiet the house was without the sounds of Jasper playing in his room or Dom singing along with the record player they'd found in the storage shed.

At least there was still music.

Tonight, she had on an old Eagles album that reminded her of childhood summers with her Aunt Sybil. Back when she was a kid, she and Hannah would swim in the lake all day and spend their evenings around the fire pit with long sticks and a bag of marshmallows, stuffing their faces while Sybil's music drifted out to them on the porch. They would go to bed with sticky fingers, staring up at the starry sky through the skylight, talking about all the adventures they would have when they were older.

Instead, she and her sister had been ripped apart, and now Hannah was in another corner of the world watching the stars wink on in a different sky, and Harley was alone.

She truly felt alone and was as relaxed as she could be given what the future held. As she tipped her beer back for the last swallow at the bottom, the red truck and the mystery fisherman were far from her nostalgic thoughts.

That's when he made his move, grabbing her from behind and shoving a needle deep into her neck, proving he was a superior predator.

Harley cried out as her muscles spasmed and her vision flooded black, but there was no one around to hear. No one but the man who grabbed her around her waist, lifting her into the air and carrying her away, leaving the music playing and the soup to burn on the stove.

## DIRTY TWISTED LOVE

# CHAPTER FOUR

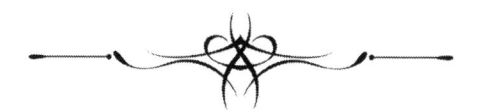

Clay

Clay Hart had spent the last two years of his career with the CIA shadowing mercenaries in Afghanistan and keeping watch over the poppy fields the CIA insisted they weren't harvesting in secret and selling to U.S. drug companies desperately in need of poppy latex. He had learned to blend in, to move about unobserved, and to become part of the shadows until the moment was right to reveal himself.

His superiors had hesitated to send a blue eyed, blond haired operative into the Middle East to "blend in" but Clay had quickly proved that their worries were groundless. He was never made. He never missed his mark. He never failed to get in, get out, get the job done, and do it all without being seen.

But Harley had seen him.

He'd felt her eyes on him as he'd bent over the bed of the truck, wondering what the fuck he was going to do if she decided to come over and say hello. He was a different man than the person she'd known, his heart empty and his soul dark from too much time spent staring into the void, but his face was the same.

She would have recognized him and then he would have had to explain himself. He would have had to come up with a lie that would convince her to drop her guard long enough for him to inject the sedative, and he wasn't sure he would have been able to pull it off.

He was a master at making lies sound like the truth, but he had never lied to someone he hated the way he hated the woman hidden under the tarp in the bed of his truck.

Clay leaned over, eyeing the lump lying motionless beneath the thick gray plastic before turning back to the moonlit ocean stretching into the distance in all directions. The sedative should keep her knocked out for at least ten hours, more than long enough for the ferry to reach Ko Pha Ngan. From there, they would take his private boat to one of the smallest of the south Thai islands, an unnamed patch of land home to one of the CIA's inoperative black sites.

Black sites—secret international prisons where the CIA locked away people they didn't want to attract attention on U.S. soil—were fewer in number than they used to be, but they were still around. This one had closed a year ago but had been left intact, ready for reopening at a moment's notice. The lights were still on, the water running, and the emergency bunker was stocked with enough canned goods to last a small prison population several months.

He and Harley should be more than comfortable.

Or at least *he* would be comfortable. Her comfort depended on how quickly she gave him what he wanted.

Clay glanced up at the night sky, lips twisting in a bitter smile. If he'd known that Harley had Jasper on the island with her, things would have gone down differently. But every still he'd captured from the bank security camera in the village had shown Harley alone. When he'd learned that she'd chartered a plane from Ko Tao to Bangkok, he had anticipated having to deal with one woman. One woman who would be easily put down with a tranquilizer dart and shuffled into the bed of his truck.

The airstrip was only for private use; so few planes came in or out that there wasn't even an air traffic controller to monitor the area. Recon on the strip had assured Clay that the only person who might observe him kidnapping Harley was the pilot waiting in the plane and he wouldn't be able to get across the field fast enough to stop Clay from driving away.

When a little blond boy had tumbled out of Harley's car, followed by a tall man with dark hair, Clay had been forced to put away his stun gun and reassess the situation. He wasn't sure how he was going to explain to the son he'd never met why they would be building a life together without his mother in the picture, but he knew he couldn't let Jasper's introduction to him involve being yanked into a truck after seeing his mother and her boyfriend collapse onto the ground.

That was the kind of thing that scarred children for life, and Clay was sure the poor kid was plenty scarred already. After being raised by a sociopath, there was no way Jasper could have survived completely intact. But he was only six years old, still young enough to get help, get healthy, and have a normal life.

Clay had only known about Jasper for six months, but six months was long enough for him to realize he wanted to give his son the world. And if not the world, then at least a chance to grow up without being haunted by the ghosts of his mother's mistakes. As soon as they were back in the States, he and Jasper would go to therapy for as long as it took to put Harley Mason and the shit she'd put them both through far behind them.

Now it was just a matter of getting Harley to cooperate.

The ferry landed a little after two in the morning. By three, Clay had Harley tucked away in the hold of his fishing boat and was headed south. They docked at the black site's hidden cove just as the sky was graying, and by sunrise, Harley was tied to a cot in one of the officer's cottages.

For the first time since carrying her to his truck, he had a chance to study her and see how she stacked up against his memories.

She was still beautiful, her long brown hair framing a face that belonged on a 1950s movie star, with a plush mouth and a chin that came to a sharp point, making her look almost feline when she smiled. She was in better shape than she'd been when they were younger—there were defined muscles on the arms stretched above her head—but still a little too thin, lending her the same air of fragility she'd always had. That delicacy had made it easy to believe her when she'd claimed that people had hurt her.

But she'd been the one doing the hurting. She was a monster, a devil with a pretty face, the kind of evil you never saw coming until your life was shattered and by then, she was already gone, moving on to her next victim.

But not this time.

This time, one way or another, Harley was going to pay for her sins.

Clay settled onto the small couch beside the bed, threaded his fingers together, and watched the morning sun creep across the white sheets, waiting for Harley to wake up and realize there was a bigger, scarier creature in the jungle.

## DIRTY TWISTED LOVE

# CHAPTER FIVE

### Harley

The first time Harley woke up, the world was blurry, her head throbbed like a finger with a splinter shoved beneath the nail, and her mouth was so dry she would have sold her soul for a drink of water. She blinked heavy lids as her head lolled first to the left—a large window with a view of palm trees and a smudge of ocean beyond—and then to the right—a man sitting on a couch.

An enormous man.

Harley swallowed, her bone-dry throat clutching at itself as she fought to focus. She made out sandy hair, a square jaw, and finally the finer details of his face. His face.

*His* face.

"Good to see you." Her words were a cross between a mumble and a croak, but it didn't matter. This was a dream, she realized with a pang of sadness. That was the only time she saw Clay, in dreams where little things like alive or dead didn't matter.

Dream Clay leaned forward, his lips moving, but she couldn't hear what he was saying. She was already being pulled back under, into a deeper, more fragmented sleep.

There she dreamed of staircases stretching into the sky with sweating glasses of water waiting at the top for her to drink them. But every time she reached the top and stretched her fingers out to close around the glistening tumbler, the stairs would flatten and she would slide down, down, down to where she'd started. She climbed the stairs again and again, her thirst growing until it was a screaming need clawing at her throat, until she wept and in her desperation smeared her own tears back into her mouth, sucking the salty wetness onto her tongue.

She woke with a moan and a shudder in her chest, her tears following her into the waking world.

"Water," she croaked, her damp lashes sticking together as she opened her eyes. Her head didn't hurt anymore, but the thirst was torturous. If this was how her captors meant to kill her, her death would be terrible, a slow descent into madness. "Please, water."

"Here," a deep voice said from beside her. "Just a sip."

Harley's head rolled to the right, her lips parting in a silent "oh." If her throat weren't so dry, she would have cried out with a sound equal to the shock of seeing a man risen from the dead.

It was Clay and this was no dream. He was here. Now. With her in this room.

He'd aged since the last time she'd seen

him. His deeply tanned skin was lightly creased around his eyes and across his forehead and he had acquired a long, jagged scar above his left temple. It was where he had been bleeding the night of the crash, the night she had touched his cold face and been certain that he was dead.

"H-how," she rasped, eyes wide as she scanned his face, searching for clues. There was something different about him, something more than the fine lines and the scar, but her fogged mind couldn't figure out what it was. "I th-thought you were dead."

"I have been," he said, holding out a cup with a straw in it. "Do you want a drink or not?"

Blinking fast, she leaned over, closing her lips around the straw and sucking greedily until Clay grabbed the top and pulled it from her mouth.

"Not too much," he said, setting the water back on the table by the bed. "You'll make yourself sick."

Harley lay back on the pillows, flexing and releasing her fingers as her thoughts raced.

Clay was alive.

Her arms were bound above her head.

Clay was alive.

She'd been kidnapped from her house.

Clay was alive.

There had been a needle in her throat and then the world had gone black.

And now she was here, wherever here was, and Clay was alive, sitting beside her bed, waiting for her to wake up.

"Wh-why…." She shook her head, trailing off as she swallowed hard, forcing the water trying to crawl up her throat back down again. "What—"

"I don't remember you being this slow on the uptake." Clay leaned in, his elbows resting on his knees. "Come on Harley, use that clever brain of yours. You know why. And you know what this is."

Her eyes went wider until the muscles ached around the sockets.

This couldn't be happening. Clay was the nicest man she'd ever met. He was laughter and thoughtfulness and long nights whispering beneath the covers like they were children breaking the rules to stay up late and tell ghost stories. He was the only man who had ever made her laugh and come at the same time, and his eyes were the first place she'd seen a reflection of herself that wasn't twisted or wrong.

He'd shown her a glimpse of a woman who was lovable. And for the first time in her life she'd dared to believe that maybe—when her revenge was complete and the bodies lying still in their graves—she could be a person like Hannah. She could be worthy of love and happiness and long sleeps without any nightmares in them.

Now, she saw that worthy person in Jasper's eyes. And now, when she looked at herself in the mirror, she saw a woman who kept her secrets close, but her son closer.

She wasn't the selfish, destructive child she'd been the night she and Clay were run off the road on their way to get married in Niagara Falls. That girl had died, but she'd left wreckage behind and wounded people prepared to take up the torch of revenge and hold it to her bare feet.

She suddenly knew why Clay had brought her here and it made her heart stutter in her chest.

"I can explain," she said, tongue slipping out to dampen her lips.

"You can explain why you framed Jackson for rape?" Clay said, the contempt in his voice making her cringe. "You can explain why you lied and convinced me that he beat you, destroying my relationship with a man who was like a brother to me?"

"It wasn't about—"

"An innocent man," Clay continued, before she could begin to explain, "who went to jail and lost everything—his career, his family, his good name—because of you. You destroyed his life, Harley. You took everything that mattered away from him. And why? To punish his father, who couldn't give two shits about his son."

Harley bit her bottom lip, fighting to think past the fear surging inside of her. She knew what was different about Clay now. His eyes didn't reflect anything anymore. They were flat, hard, and utterly lacking in empathy. She had a barren place inside of her where their love had once lived, but Clay had a hellscape, a nightmare world inhabited by demons born from the special breed of hatred one can only feel for a person he or she once loved.

"And I believed you for years," he continued in a softer voice. "I believed you loved me and that you'd died an innocent woman who'd had her life, and her chance at happiness, stolen away from her. Stolen away from me."

Her throat ached. "Please, Clay, let me at least try to explain."

"But I know the truth now. And I have enough evidence to put you in jail for the rest of your life." He placed a hand on her forehead with enough pressure to send a fresh rush of fear washing through her. "I know you've been helping Marlowe Reynolds smuggle drugs inside your sculptures. I have pictures, audio, and your fingerprints on the bags you sealed inside the plaster. All I have to do is press send on an email to my department head and I'll have a warrant to take you in."

"No, you can't," she said, knowing it was a stupid thing to say the moment the words left her mouth.

But she wasn't thinking clearly. All she could think about was Jasper out in the world alone and her behind bars unable to see her son ever again.

Clay's hand slid into her hair, fisting in the strands at the top of her scalp as he leaned closer, growling his next words into her face, "You don't tell me what I can or can't do. You don't manipulate people or make up the rules to the game. Not anymore."

He released her and sat back, continuing in a more controlled voice, "From now on, your job is to give me what I want when I want it. That's your purpose and the quicker you get used to it, the sooner this will be over."

"So what do you want?" she said, anger rising inside of her. "To punish me, hurt me? Go ahead. I know I deserve it for the things I did, but I'm not that person anymore. I swear I'm not. And I have people depending on me, innocent people who need me to stay out of jail."

"Like our son," he said, knocking the wind out of her. "I know about Jasper. I saw him get onto the plane with your friend. I hope you said a meaningful goodbye because that was the last time you're ever going to see him."

"No!" For the first time since she woke up, her voice was strong. "You can't. He needs me!"

Clay's lip curled. "He doesn't need you. I wouldn't wish you on my worst enemy, let alone my son."

"He does need me," she insisted, anger and fear pumping through her, making her tremble. "Jasper loves me and I love him. We're a family. I swear to you, Clay, I love him more than anything in the world. Everything I've done since the day he was born has been for him."

"For him." Clay smiled, an ugly smile that made her feel smaller than she had in a long time. "You've been smuggling drugs for one of the most dangerous men in the world for your son? Surely even you realize that doesn't sound like something a real mother would do.

Real mothers go out of their way to protect their children from danger. They don't offer it an engraved invitation."

"I never told Marlowe about Jasper. He doesn't even know I have a son," she said, tears rising in her eyes. "I've done my best to protect him. If I'd had a choice, I would have been out a long time ago. I didn't know the way Marlowe worked when it started. I was only planning to work for him for a year, maybe two, just until I could make enough money to—"

"You had money. I know who your father is." He shook his head, a sharp burst of laughter escaping his lips. "Did you have fun that summer, pretending to be a cocktail waitress and slumming with Jackson and me? Fucking both of us while you turned the men who loved you against each other?"

"This isn't about you," she said with a sob, sending the tears in her eyes spilling down her cheeks. "Or Jackson. Or me. Or the ugliness in the past. This is about a smart, sweet, amazing little boy who loves and needs his mother. You can't take me away from him.

You can't, Clay, or you'll be as terrible a person as I was back then."

His eyes flashed with cold rage, but Harley couldn't seem to stop words from streaming out of her mouth.

"No, you'll be worse," she said, sniffing hard. "Because you weren't raised by a mother who couldn't stand the sight of you and a father who encouraged you to be a vicious piece of shit. You had parents who loved you and laughed with you and told you how wonderful you were. You were whole to start with, Clay, you didn't have to learn—"

Before she realized he was moving, he was on the bed, looming over her with his hand around her neck.

"And then you destroyed me!" he shouted, the hatred in his eyes making her tears flow faster as his grip tightened, wrenching a gagging sound from her throat. "You killed the person I was, you poisonous cunt! You are toxic and if you think I'm going to let you so much as speak to Jasper through the bars of a prison cell, you're out of your fucking mind."

Harley squirmed beneath him, her body writhing as her vision grayed around the edges and the backs of her eyes began to pulse.

Years ago, she could never have imagined herself and Clay in a position like this. No matter how angry he might have been, Clay wasn't the kind of person to take out his rage on another person, especially a woman tied to a bed, helpless to defend herself. But he wasn't that man anymore. He was a monster, a monster she had created and now he was back from the dead, crawled out of his grave to take retribution.

They said karma was a bitch, but at that moment Harley knew karma was a devil with the face of the man you loved, slowly choking the life from your body as the world went dark.

DIRTY TWISTED LOVE

# CHAPTER SIX

Clay

Clay forced his hand from Harley's throat and stumbled away from the bed, his arms shaking at his sides.

What the fuck?

What the fuck had he almost done?

He'd brought Harley here to force her to tell him where Jasper was and facilitate the handoff between whoever had the boy and

Clay's people. This wasn't about hurting her—at least not any more than he had to—let alone killing her.

But hearing the self-righteous note in her voice and seeing her cry as if *she* were the one who deserved pity and compassion, he'd just…lost it.

She was still breathing—she was unconscious, but he could see her chest rising and falling—but if he had kept his hand at her throat for another minute, maybe two…

However long he'd had left before he strangled a woman to death with his bare hands, it had been too fucking close. He never should have let himself lose control. He had to get out of here, away from her, and pull his shit together. As much as he hated to admit it, she was right—if he stooped to her level, he would be no better than she was.

Grabbing his hat off the dining table in the corner, he pushed through the screen door and out into the increasingly hot morning. Shoving the hat on his head—no need to make it easy for any drones cruising the area to see his face; he would have his ass handed to him if his superiors learned he was here without permission—he headed for the trees behind the officer bungalows.

Once he was in the shade, concealed by the thick leaves of the rainforest that covered most of this island, he braced his hands against a thick, softly peeling trunk and dropped his head. He closed his eyes but opened them again almost immediately. When he closed his eyes, all he saw was Harley's tear-stained face and the way the veins had stood out on her forehead just before she'd lost consciousness.

He had killed before—in combat and in more shadowy ways in his work for the CIA—but those people had been strangers. Strangers who had signed up to fight for an opposing military force, or who had a dossier of crimes a mile long. He had never killed someone he knew personally, let alone someone he'd fucked so many times he could still remember the little sounds she made when she was about to go over, her pussy squeezing his cock until he thought he'd die from how right it felt to be inside of her.

*You didn't fuck her; you made love to her.*

*You made love to her and asked her to marry you, and if that truck hadn't come out of nowhere, she would have been your wife.*

Clay pulled in a deep breath and let it out through clenched teeth, hating how wild he still felt. He couldn't dwell on the way things had been with Harley—how she could make him laugh until his stomach cramped, or the way her smell had swirled around him as they moved together, making love all night with the windows open and the sea breeze blowing across their sweat-slick skin.

She still smelled the same. Even with the sour scent of sweat and fear rising from her body, he could catch the notes of citrus, sea salt, and eternal summer lingering in her hair. For a moment, when he'd been holding the glass for her to drink and the breeze had blown through the window, the smell of her had tugged at something low in his body.

He hadn't gotten hard, but he'd definitely gotten thicker. And that was enough to scare the shit out of him.

He couldn't believe she still had the power

to make him respond. After all he'd been through, after all the pain and rage and having six years with his son stolen away from him, he should be immune. But he wasn't. He still wanted her as much as he hated her. He could still look at her long legs and imagine them wrapped around him while he sank into her softness.

But it would be different now. Now, he wouldn't make love to her. Now, he would get off on taking something she didn't care to give, from taking what he wanted and not giving a shit if it brought her pain.

In fact, pain would be good. He wanted her to hurt.

He had never touched a woman in anger and until this moment the thought of taking a woman against her will had sickened him. Rape was for useless, pathetic bullies who needed to violate weaker people in order to feel powerful. But the thought of Harley beneath him, tears streaming down her cheeks as he fucked her hard enough to make her breasts bounce wildly on her chest didn't repulse him. It made his balls tighten and heat spread through his pelvis.

Before he could push the sickening mental image from his mind he was rock hard, his cock straining the khaki shorts he'd changed into on the ferry.

With a groan, Clay turned and leaned back against the tree, staring up at the tiny black birds dancing through the canopy. He tried to clear his mind of the twisted shit—to think of how physically exhausted he was after almost twenty-four hours without sleep or how many things could go wrong before he had Jasper in a plane with him headed back to Maryland—but his thoughts were a pit bull straining against a leash.

They kept coming back to Harley, to her smell and her arms bound to the headboard and how much he wanted to rip the filmy white shirt she was wearing in two and get his mouth on her tits.

*Fuck.* Now he was even harder, his balls aching and his swollen shaft desperate for relief.

With a soft curse, he loosened the drawstring on his shorts and reached inside.

He took himself in hand, wrapping his fingers around his feverish cock and squeezing. He let his eyes slide closed as he began to work himself up and down, using the pre-cum welling at his tip for lubrication. He had to get off—preferably to something other than the ugliness swirling through his head—and get his focus back in the right place.

Head falling back against the tree, he thought of Adeleh, the Persian woman he'd lived with for a few months in the Gostan Valley. Adeleh was one of the loveliest women he'd ever seen, a beauty with full breasts that overflowed his hands, plush, rounded hips, and dark eyes so sexy just a glance across a darkened room was almost enough to make him come. She was the opposite of Harley: dark to her light, curvy to Harley's boyish figure, and as kind and generous as Harley was intense and demanding.

Fucking Adeleh had been nothing but a pleasure, a way to ease the loneliness he felt being stationed in a foreign country and for her to begin to overcome her grief over losing her husband. Love had never been in the cards—his heart was a wasteland and hers too broken to allow that depth of emotion—but they'd had passion in spades.

As Clay's hand moved faster, he thought of their last night together, the way Adeleh had straddled him, positioning his cock at her entrance and slowly lowering her hips until he was encased in her heat. He remembered the way her long black hair had formed a curtain around their faces as she leaned down to kiss him and the feel of her breasts heavy in his hands, seeming to grow even heavier as he squeezed and rolled her nipples. He remembered the way her breath had rushed out across his lips as she moved faster, riding his cock with her hands braced on his chest.

He was thrusting into his hand, imagining that it was Adeleh's slick body, when the images flickering behind his closed lids shifted. Suddenly it wasn't black hair spilling around him, but silken brown curls.

Adeleh's solid weight vanished, replaced by Harley's lighter frame.

*"You know this is what you want," Harley said,*

*the muscles in her arms flexing as she gripped the headboard above him. "You want to be so deep inside of me I'll feel you for days."*

*"Shut your mouth."* He rolled them over, taking control with a sharp thrust into her heat, drawing a moan from low in her throat as the head of his cock butted against the end of her channel.

*Fuck, she felt so good, so tight and wet, her inner walls fitting around him like a glove.*

*"I don't want to shut my mouth." She locked her ankles behind his back and clenched her thigh muscles, pulling him impossibly deeper. "You know I like to talk."*

*"I'm not in the mood to listen," he snapped, grabbing her legs behind the knees and forcing them up and out, until she was spread wide, completely vulnerable to him as he withdrew and slammed his cock back inside her, sending pain flickering across her features. "So keep quiet. Or I'll find something to shut you up."*

*"God, Clay." Harley arched beneath him, grimacing as he fucked her so hard the flesh of her thighs rippled as he drove home again and again, the tension in his body building until the base of his spine burned and every nerve in his body was crackling with*

*electricity. "Yes. Fuck me. Use me. Hurt me."*

*With a growl of frustration he pulled out and flipped her over onto her stomach, roughly kneeing her thighs apart before shoving into her from behind. As soon as he was back inside her tight cunt, he wrapped his hand around her neck, covering her mouth as he brought his lips to her ear.*

*"You don't speak," he whispered, his free arm banding around her waist, holding her captive as he thrust into her, hard and deep. "You don't deserve a voice."*

*She moaned, her breath warm on his hand as she spread her thighs wider. Clenching his jaw, Clay accepted the silent invitation. He rode her hard, pounding into her until she whimpered and his balls ached from slamming into her pussy at the end of each thrust. But he didn't pull back; he held her tighter and fucked her harder.*

*Harder, harder, until she screamed into his hand.*

*She screamed and bucked beneath him, her cunt clutching at his dick, coating him with a gush of slickness as she tumbled over. He joined her with a guttural sound, his cock jerking as he came so hard his chest felt like it was turning inside out.*

Clay opened his eyes to see his cock

thrusting through his own fist, the thick length pulsing as his cum splashed out to coat the leaves at his feet. He bit his lip, fighting to stay silent as he jerked and pulsed, riding out the last waves of the best orgasm he'd had in years.

In *years*.

Fantasizing about fucking Harley had gotten him off harder than being with a beautiful, sweet woman who he considered a real friend, the kind he would drop everything and fly back to Iran to help if she were ever in trouble. He hadn't raped Harley in his fantasy, but he wasn't messed up enough to consider that a victory. At least not yet.

No, he wasn't a monster, but if he stayed on this island alone with Harley Mason long enough, he would become one.

The real Harley hated him for trying to take her son away. She wouldn't give consent, let alone spread her legs and silently ask for more. If he gave in to his twisted longing for her, she would fight him. And then he would find out if he was the kind of man who would take a woman against her will.

He swallowed hard as he tucked himself back into his boxer briefs. He didn't want to find out if that kind of evil lived inside of him. He didn't want to be that man and he refused to let Harley bring more misery into his life.

Which meant he had to get what he needed from her and get rid of her as quickly as possible, no lingering on this island, no taking his time coaxing the truth from her.

As much as he hated to bargain with the devil, it might be best to make a deal. Better to offer her a reward in exchange for her cooperation than to spend a month or more here alone with her, slowly losing his mind from a mix of wanting and hating.

A plan forming, Clay made his way through the forest to a hidden beach surrounded by thick foliage where he stripped to the skin and dove into the cool waves.

As his body sank below the surface and the ocean swept by overhead, Clay let the salt water wash away the evidence of his release, wishing the sea could wash away his sick longing for Harley as easily.

# CHAPTER SEVEN

## Harley

Harley woke up in a rush, her heart pounding and her body electrified by fear. Her eyes flew open, blinking fast as an unfamiliar ceiling and ceiling fan swam into view. She swallowed hard, wincing at the aching in her throat, wondering what had awoken her and why she was so terrified.

As the bruised flesh around her windpipe

contracted, it all came rushing back.

Clay.

His hand at her throat.

The world going black and the certainty that she was about to die.

To die without seeing Jasper again, without being able to tell him she loved him, or without having the chance to write that letter she'd always meant to write: the one that thanked him for transforming her heart and giving her the most beautiful years of her life. She'd started the letter a hundred times, but it seemed dangerous to write words meant only to be read if she died before her son was old enough to have the conversation in person. It was like writing a will. She'd never done that either, not wanting to tempt fate by preparing for the worst.

It was magical thinking at its worst and she suddenly wished she'd put it in writing that she wanted Hannah to take Jasper, on the off chance that Dominic decided not to honor her wishes or if he were intercepted by her father before he could reach Hannah in Samoa. If she got out of here alive, the first thing on the agenda was finding Jasper and finding a place to hide. The second would be getting a will drawn up and arrangements made to protect Jasper from the madman his biological father had become.

Her head rolled to one side and then the other, searching for signs of life, relaxing only slightly when she saw that she was alone.

Clay wasn't here, but he would be back, she had no doubt about that. And when he returned he might decide to finish the job he'd started. She had to think and think fast. It didn't matter that a part of her would always be in love with the man she'd known; Clay wasn't that person anymore. He was her enemy and had to be treated as such.

In the old days, that would have meant total destruction, annihilation from the inside out, and maybe a few bombs planted in his everyday life for him to stumble across later. Now, it meant running as far and as fast as she was able and being prepared to hide so well Clay would never find her again.

But she wasn't going anywhere as long as she was tied to this bed.

First things first. Even in times like these, it was important to attack obstacles one at a time.

Flexing her arms, she pulled herself as close to upright as she could get with her hands bound to the top of the headboard. The bed was constructed of cheap-looking wood, but it was strong enough that she wouldn't have a chance of breaking the slat she was secured to with muscle power alone. But Clay hadn't bound her feet. If she could find something to use to cut through the rope, she might be able to drag the twin bed across the room to reach it.

She let her eyes sweep the small space. To her left were a large window and a screen door leading outside. In the corner was a table for two, and directly in front of the bed sat a large bureau that took up most of the wall. In the opposite corner was a closed door she suspected led to the bathroom and to her right a small couch. Behind it was a kitchenette with two cabinets up top, an electric range, and a sink all crammed together.

It was a tiny efficiency situation, but meals were clearly intended to be cooked there. And where meals were prepared there would be silverware—and most importantly for her, knives.

She let her tongue slip out to dampen her lips, deciding if she were caught in the middle of her escape attempt, she could tell Clay that she was just trying to make it to the bathroom. She should have to go by now. It was only dehydration that was preventing her from being in serious discomfort.

Glancing back toward the door, making sure there was still no sign of Clay, she scooted to the edge of the bed and twisted to the left, sliding her feet onto the floor. Her knees trembled, unsteady after so many hours of disuse, but after a moment her bones found their centers and her bare feet adjusted to the cool temperature of the tile. She didn't know where her sandals had gone, but she didn't need shoes to escape. She'd spent half her life on the island barefoot anyway. All she needed was to get her arms free and get out of this cottage. From there she would find a way to get to help.

Strengthened by the thought, she gave an experimental tug, heart lifting when the bed slid toward her. It wasn't secured to the floor. It was heavy, but it wasn't far to the kitchen and there was only the small couch in her way. She would be able to make it across the room in a few minutes.

She leaned over, taking a long drink of the water by the bed, wincing as her throat muscles protested the work she was forcing them to do. But she was still dying of thirst and as soon as she was free, she wanted to be ready to run.

After her drink, she tugged the bed away from the wall and around the bedside table. A few minutes later she had dragged it past the couch and into the tiny kitchen. She stopped a few feet from the drawers, heart racing as she reached out with one bare foot and gripped the drawer pull with her toes. She fumbled the first time, but the second time she managed to slide the drawer open and was rewarded with the rattle of silverware inside.

Biting back a cry of celebration, she pulled

the bed frame closer to the open drawer. She glanced down, spirits sinking when she saw only a few rusted forks, spoons, and butter knives, and one dented steak knife that looked like it had seen sharper days. But it was all she had and thankfully the rope Clay had used looked like it would be easy to cut. It was soft, silky rope, not anything course or covered with a protective coating.

She bent low, straining against her bonds as she reached for the knife with her mouth. It took a few tries and she banged her forehead on the counter once when she dropped the knife halfway to standing, but finally she had the wooden handle of the steak knife between her teeth.

Glancing back toward the door, silently thanking whatever force was keeping Clay away from the cottage, she crawled back onto the mattress on her knees, facing her hands. The rope was twisted now that she'd reversed her position—her right wrist pinned beneath her left and the rope cutting deeper into her flesh—but she could reach her left wrist easily. All she had to do was get through the rope and she would be able to free her other hand.

Using her tongue to flip the knife over, she positioned the blade and clenched her jaw, teeth digging into the handle as she bent over, bringing the blade to the rope. She sawed back and forth with short, sharp jerks of her head. Almost immediately, she was rewarded with frayed, fuzzy strands of white fluffing around her mouth.

She got through most of the first loop and moved on to the second, hoping that if she hacked far enough through all three lengths of rope she would be able to squirm her hand free without risking cutting herself with the rusty knife. She couldn't remember the last time she'd had a tetanus shot and it might be a long time before she was able to get to a doctor.

She didn't even know if she was still on Ko Tao. She'd been unconscious for at least one night, maybe more. Clay could have taken her all the way to Bangkok in that amount of time, but judging by the smell of the breeze rushing in from outside, she would bet she was still on the islands.

But it might be a different island, one without a large local population and no medical clinic. Still, there had to be a way back to civilization. Clay had brought her here somehow. With a little luck, she would be able to use that same method to get herself out. She could hotwire a car, drive a boat, and fly a plane. She was uniquely equipped to survive something like this, a fact she kept repeating to herself as she hacked through the second length of rope and started on the third.

Whatever knot Clay had used, it was elaborate. Each length of rope encircled her wrist separately and was secured before being joined to a more intricate knot between her wrists. She was halfway through the third rope and already planning her dash to the front door when she heard footsteps on the gravel path outside.

For a panicked second, she froze before clenching her teeth and sawing more frantically. She cut through the last rope and into her skin, leaving a deep gash that immediately began to fill with red. But if she could get out of here before Clay got inside it would be worth risking a case of lockjaw.

Grabbing the knife in her now free hand, ignoring the blood running down her arm, she quickly sawed her way through the ropes binding her right wrist. By the time she saw a flash of movement outside the screen door, she was already running for the bathroom, praying there was a window she could crawl out of.

"Harley!" Clay's shout came from behind her. "Stop!"

*Yeah right.*

*How about I run like hell instead?*

# CHAPTER EIGHT

Harley

Harley slammed the door behind her and locked it, sobbing with relief as she saw that the bathroom became a laundry room. And on the other side of the stackable laundry machine was a door leading outside.

As she dashed through the small space, she grabbed the hand towel hanging near the sink and wrapped it around her bloody wrist. The wound was definitely starting to sting, but she was so high on adrenaline she barely felt it.

Breathing hard from a combination of terror and going too long without food or much water, she shoved through the door, emerging into another sunny day in paradise. It seemed wrong for the sun to be shining on a day like this, but Mother Nature had proven that she didn't give any more of a damn about human drama than humans gave about her polar ice caps.

Harley froze, taking in her surroundings as her eyes adjusted to the bright light. She was in the middle of a clearing, near several other cottages, on the other side of which lay thick rainforest, much denser than anything on Ko Tao. She was definitely on a different island, but she didn't have time to wonder which one.

She had to move, hide!

She broke for the forest, sprinting for all she was worth, refusing to look back over her shoulder, even when she heard Clay shout again and the thud of his footfalls following her across the grass. She clenched her jaw and pumped her arms harder at her sides, silently thanking Dom for forcing her into the best shape of her life. If she ever saw him again, she was going to kiss him senseless, and vow never to skip abs and legs again.

And she was going to see him again. Him and Jasper.

She hit the cool shade of the forest and took a hard left, veering away from the dirt trail leading to the right. The trees were closer together and it was harder going with sticks and rocks digging into the bottoms of her bare feet, but it would be harder for Clay to follow her this way. If she stayed on open ground, he would catch her sooner or later. She was barefoot, weak, and had much shorter legs.

But if she could get to one of the thicker parts of the forest—maybe find a bamboo grove or a swampy area with water to sink beneath—she might be able to lay low long enough for Clay to lose her trail.

"Stop, Harley," he shouted, sounding close but not dangerously so, not yet. "The longer you run, the worse it's going to be for you when I catch you."

*Worse than nearly choking me to death?* But she didn't speak; she couldn't afford to waste her breath.

She ran faster, weaving around trees as she followed the gentle slope of the hill down into a stiller place, where the air was thick and humid and the sea breeze was a distant memory. Sweat dripped down her forehead to sting into her eyes; she blinked it away and pushed harder. Clay was losing ground. His footfalls were farther away now and a hiding place was in sight.

At the base of the hill was a vast patch of thick, prickly-looking bushes interspersed with bright green ferns that stretched all the way to a moss-covered bluff on the far side of the small valley. If she could get deep enough into the press of growth and lie still, it would be nearly impossible for Clay to find her.

She reached the edge of the low-growing shrubs and dove to the ground, scrambling forward on her hands and knees beneath the thick foliage. Her hands sank into the moist soil and the sharp edges of roots sticking up through the earth tore the skin on her knees, but she kept crawling as fast as she could, putting ground between her and Clay. She heard him curse, followed by the sound of brush behind violently swatted aside, and dared to hope that her plan was going to work.

Without a machete, there was no way Clay would be able to walk through the dense growth and he was so large it would be a tight fit for him low to the ground. Harley was half his size and as the brush thickened, she was forced onto her forearms in order to squeeze between the increasingly close trunks of the bushes. If she were doing anything but running for her life, she would be fighting a panic attack.

She hated tight spaces. She and Hannah both suffered from claustrophobia. Hannah blamed hers on the time Harley had accidentally locked her in their secret attic hideout when they were kids. Harley blamed her own on the night she'd spent inside her ex-boyfriend's trunk in high school.

She had broken up with Kerry—casually mentioning that she'd already invited her new man to her pool party next weekend and that Kerry should consider himself uninvited. He responded by throwing her in his trunk, slamming it closed, and shouting that he was going to drive the car into a lake and watch her drown.

She spent the next five hours sweating and shaking with fear as he drove around the back roads, stopping often enough that she was in a constant state of terror, certain the car was about to roll into the water. Finally, just after dawn, he let her out on the front lawn of their private prep school, about thirty minutes after she'd lost control of her bladder. He took pictures of her mascara-streaked face and the piss stains on the front of her jeans and then drove off with her purse in his backseat.

She walked the ten miles home, flipping off the one sweet little old lady who stopped to ask if she was okay. She didn't want anyone to see her like that and asking for help would have been admitting that she needed it. Instead, she stewed the entire way home, plotting the perfect revenge for Kerry—which she pulled off without a hitch, without regret, and without getting caught, just the way her father had taught her.

Back then, there was nothing she'd hated more than being vulnerable. To be vulnerable was to be like her mother, a woman who had let a man destroy her without even putting up a fight.

But right now, she would welcome help with open arms. She would even welcome her father or Marlowe waiting at the edge of the forest with a gun. Sure, they were devils, but they were the devils she knew.

She didn't know Clay, not anymore, and that scared her as much as anything else. If he caught her again, she had no idea how to make him dance to her tune. Here there was only Clay's music and her blood flowing out to coat the dance floor.

Stifling a whimper as a root poked at her wound through the towel, she wriggled into a shadowed place between four larger bushes and curled into a tight ball. She tucked her chin to her chest and fought to slow her breath, not wanting to give Clay any clue where she was hiding. Her ears strained and after a moment she heard a soft grunt and another rustle of leaves from far to her left. It didn't sound like he'd made it far through the bushes and she couldn't see any sign of his feet.

She bit her lip as she turned to gauge how far it was to the bluff on the other side of the brush. Would it be better to keep moving and put even more distance between her and Clay? Surely she could find another place to hide—the forest was ridiculously dense—and maybe that place wouldn't have beetles the size of her hand crawling over her bare legs and mosquitoes swarming around her bloodied knees.

And even more importantly, Clay would have no idea where to start looking for her.

Trusting her gut, she rolled back over and belly crawled slowly through the last of the dense bushes, trying not to make a sound. After only a few minutes, the small trunks began to grow farther apart again as the shrubs thinned near the edge of the grove.

She came back onto her hands and knees, but kept her slower pace, not wanting Clay to see her when she emerged.

She was nearly to the wide, leaf-scattered stones at the base of the cliff, where enough sun filtered through the leaves that she was grateful that her hair was no longer sunlight-catching blond, when footfalls sounded from her left. She jerked her head to the side to see Clay sprinting straight for her.

He'd gone around the bushes, not through!

With a strangled cry, Harley lurched to her feet and turned to run only to skid to a stop when something long and dark sprung up from the ground in front of her.

She flinched then froze, eyes going wide as an ominous hissing filled the air.

DIRTY TWISTED LOVE

# CHAPTER NINE

Clay

The snake was a king cobra, at least twelve feet long, reared up on its belly with its hooded head even with Harley's chest. Thankfully, she'd had the sense to stop running, but the animal clearly still felt threatened. It could strike at any second and Harley wouldn't have time to blink, let alone dodge the attack, before the snake's fangs were in her.

"That's a king cobra," he said in a soft, soothing voice. "One of the most venomous snakes in the world."

"I know," she whispered, summoning another long, witch's hiss from the creature.

"Don't talk," he warned gently. "Just listen. I'm going to come up very slowly behind you. Don't turn to look at me and don't make any sudden movements until I tell you to."

Keeping an eye on the snake, Clay slowly stripped off his white tee shirt and clenched it lightly in his hand. He eased a foot closer and then another, his steps silent on the warm stones where the cobra had been sunning itself. "Now in just a second, I'm going to throw my shirt on the ground just ahead of you to your left. As soon as you see it in your peripheral vision, turn and run toward me as fast as you can. I'll get out of your way and follow behind you. The snake should attack the shirt and give us enough time to get away before it can recover for a second strike."

"And if it doesn't?" she said, so softly he could barely hear her.

"It will," he said with more confidence than he felt. He'd read up on the wildlife of the island while he was preparing the facility for his captive, but until now, surviving an encounter with a king cobra had been purely theoretical knowledge. "Just don't hesitate. Not even for a second. I know you may believe otherwise right now, but I don't want you dead."

Her shoulders stiffened, but she didn't speak or give any other sign as to whether or not she believed him.

Clay inched closer, his gut telling him he should be prepared just in case Harley decided not to follow directions. Not following directions was one of her strong suits, and one of the things he'd loved about her once upon a time.

But this wasn't a locked gate at a private beach; this was life and death. King cobras dispensed an insane amount of venom into the bloodstream, the quantity ensuring most people who were bitten died within minutes, long before they could reach medical help.

There was antivenin in the infirmary back

at the installation, but it would take at least ten minutes to get there. They would never make it in time.

If Harley didn't do exactly as he said, chances were she would die.

It wasn't until right now, seeing her facing down a snake longer than the both of them put together that he realized he didn't want her to die. He wanted his son and he wanted to never have to see this woman, who made him so aware of his own capacity for ugliness and evil, ever again, but he didn't want her dead.

"On three, Harley," he said, slowly drawing back his arm. "Just do exactly as I said and you're going to be fine. One." He stepped a little closer. "Two." His entire arm tensed, ready to throw the shirt far enough to the left that the snake wouldn't be able to shift directions easily. "Three!"

Everything happened at once—he threw the shirt, the snake leapt into the air, its powerful body flying at the scrap of cotton with fangs bared, and Harley made a break for the other side of the cliff, running in the opposite direction from where she'd been told to run.

But Clay was ready for her. She barely made it two steps before he grabbed her around the waist, hauling her against him as he turned and ran.

It was an awkward position—Harley dangling from one arm as he pumped hard with the other—but the knowledge of how fast cobras could move lent him the adrenaline rush to make it work. He kept running, ignoring Harley's grunted shout to be put down and the uncomfortable strain on his muscles until he was on the other side of the grove of thorn bushes. Only then did he glance back, his grip on Harley relaxing as he saw the cobra fleeing in the opposite direction, up into the mossy stones of the cliff.

"No you don't," he said as Harley squirmed free and made a break for the top of the ridge. He caught up with her easily, grabbing her hips and spinning her around before bending low enough to flip her over his shoulder. "No more running away."

"Put me down," she panted, pummeling his lower back with her fists.

"Not a chance, now behave yourself," he said, swatting her bottom hard enough to make her flinch and cry out. "If you bruise my kidneys on the way back, I'll take it out on your ass later."

She stiffened but stopped hitting him and a few moments passed in silence as he circled the brush and started back toward the trail, doing his best not to think about Harley bent over his knees with her bare ass in the air. He had never been into that sort of thing, but he liked the idea of reddening Harley's ass as punishment for running away from him.

He could imagine the way her muscles would lock tight from a combination of shame and discomfort. He could almost see the red welts his hand would leave behind and hear the way she would cry out as he took her punishment further, sliding his fingers between her thighs, playing with her until she was wet and squirming and hating herself for responding to his touch.

"You can put me down," Harley said,

interrupting his fantasy. But it was too late. His cock was already hard, trapped at an uncomfortable angle by his boxer briefs. "I can walk. I won't try to run away again."

"How dumb do you think I am?" he asked, tightening his grip on the back of her legs.

"I don't think you're dumb," she said. "Honestly, I'm too tired to run anymore. I haven't had any food since lunch yesterday and I—"

"Speaking of dumb," he interrupted, quickening his pace, hoping physical exertion would help banish the carnal hunger pumping through his veins. "I can't believe you would rather take your chances with a king cobra than do what I told you to do."

"You shouldn't be surprised," she said in a weary voice. "You already proved that you might kill me. The cobra's intentions were still up in the air."

"If I hadn't grabbed you, you would be dead right now," he said, but her words sent a fresh burst of self-hatred rushing through him.

He had lost control and then lost his focus,

forgetting that leaving someone like Harley tied to a bed wasn't nearly enough to ensure she would stay put. He had to pull his shit together and treat her the way he would treat any dangerous suspect during an interrogation. She wasn't a pretty, helpless, petite woman; she was a sociopath, and he'd been a fool to forget it, even for an hour.

Harley's breath rushed out in a sound that was almost a laugh. "So you want me to thank you? Is that it?"

"Of course not," he said as he stepped back onto the trail and the cottages came into sight. "I know you're incapable of gratitude. Or any other normal human emotion."

"Fuck you," she growled, her fist slamming into his ass. "You don't know what I'm capable of. You don't know me anymore!"

Rage rushing through him, Clay flipped her back onto her feet, grabbing her around the upper arms and leaning down to whisper his next words into her flushed face. "And you don't know me, and don't you forget it."

"I won't," she said, eyes glittering as she held his gaze. "I've got plenty of bruises to remember the new you by."

"You can always have more," he snapped.

Her lips stretched in a mean smile. "Lovely. That's just what Jasper needs, a father in his life to teach him how to abuse women."

"You're not a woman, you're a criminal."

"So are you!" she shouted, standing up straighter, her arm muscles flexing beneath his hands. "You kidnapped me and nearly strangled me to death."

"Keep talking," he said through gritted teeth, fighting the insane urge to shove his tongue between her lips and silence her with a kiss, "and I'll rethink the pain reliever I was going to give you."

"Fuck your pain reliever. And fuck you." Her breath rushed out as her gaze flicked from his eyes to his lips and back again.

That hint of awareness was all it took to send him over the edge.

Fisting his hand in her hair, he crushed his mouth to hers, making a sound somewhere between a groan and a growl as she opened for him and her tongue darted out to wage war with his own. Their tongues writhed against each other, fighting for supremacy, as their lips pressed so tight together he could feel her teeth bruising his lips as they fell to the grass. He rolled on top of her, grinding his erection between her legs as she bucked into him, both of them making animalistic sounds of rage and lust that drove him even wilder.

Her fingernails clawed into his bare skin, leaving scratch marks behind as he gripped her breast through her shirt and squeezed hard enough to make her gasp into his mouth.

"No, fuck you," he mumbled before pulling her bottom lip between his teeth and biting down, summoning a pained, pleasured sound from low in her throat as he released it. "I'm going to fuck you, you evil bitch. And you're going to come on my cock knowing you spread your legs for the man who is going to ruin your life."

# CHAPTER TEN

Clay

Clay pulled back, reaching for the top of her shirt, fisting his hands in the gauzy fabric and ripping it in two. She was wearing some sort of tank top underneath, but before he could rip it free, she slapped him—hard, her hand connecting with his jaw with enough force to make it ache.

"You don't get to do this," she hissed.

"You don't get to decide how I pay for what I've done!"

She reached clawed hands for his eyes, but he captured her wrists, pinning them above her head. He slammed his mouth over hers, fucking her with his tongue as he kneed her legs apart and settled between them, riding her hard through their clothes. He shifted control of both of her wrists to his left hand and used his right to pull her tank top down, freeing her breasts.

He continued to ravage her mouth, refusing to give her any spare breath to use against him, as he pinched and rolled her tight little nipples. He waited until he felt her begin to grind against him, seeking relief from the maddening tension building between them, before he reached for the close of her shorts with both hands. He ripped the fabric in two, popping the button and tearing the zipper, not caring that he was destroying the only thing she had to wear.

He didn't care about anything but getting his cock inside her and fucking her until she knew that he owned her—body and soul.

He shoved his hand down the front of her shorts and panties and drove two fingers in and up, pulse spiking as he felt how wet she was. "Fuck, Harley."

She cried out, arching into his hand, her body gushing fresh heat onto his fingers even as she raked her nails down his chest. "Get off of me!"

"You don't want me to get off." He captured one of her dangerous hands and pinned it to the ground, holding her gaze as he fucked her with his fingers. "*You* want to get off. You're about to come on my hand. You're hot and wet and dripping for me because you know this is how you deserve to get fucked. You deserve to get taken here in the dirt."

With an incoherent sound of rage, she slapped him again. But it was her left hand this time and she was too distracted to put much force behind the blow. Her breath was coming so fast her breasts were rocking on her chest, her tight nipples pinching even tighter in the breeze blowing in from the ocean.

She was going to come any second and it was going to make her furious. The knowledge was enough to make Clay's cock throb.

"Come," he said, smiling at her as he brought his thumb to her clit, rubbing her as he continued to fuck her with his hand. "Come you worthless bitch."

Crying out in what sounded like agony, she came, her pussy squeezing his fingers tight. She came gasping for air, sobbing and cursing as her cream gushed out to coat his hand until he could smell her salty sweetness on the air and the last of his capacity for rational thought left him in a rush of raw hunger. He needed to be inside her, needed to replace his fingers with his cock and ride her until she screamed.

"Stop," she shouted as he pulled her shorts and panties down her legs. "We don't have protection!"

She rolled over, trying to crawl away, but he was on her in a second, pinning her, belly down on the grass, as he shoved his shorts down far enough to free his cock.

"Pull out before you come," she snapped. "Do you hear me?"

He growled low in his throat in response. He was beyond words or compassion. He needed his dick in her, needed it like he'd never needed anything in his life. He was wild with it, bestial, ravenous.

He was drowning in his own lust and there was only one thing that could bring him back to the surface.

His bared teeth pressed against Harley's neck, he roughly kneed her thighs apart. She squirmed beneath him, rocking against his cock, feeding the madness. He threaded his hands under her arms, gripping her shoulders from the front, holding her in place as he drove frantically between her legs. He missed her entrance the first several thrusts, but finally his cock found her wet heat and he rammed home.

She moaned as he plunged to the end of her, but he moaned louder, a sound of deliverance that echoed through the air as he began to fuck her like an animal. His arms were iron banded around her body and his spine curled tightly as he thrust deeper, harder, crying out through gritted teeth as he pistoned in and out. He was no longer a man; he was a beast filled with the primal need to fuck the woman beneath him.

"I hate you," Harley cried out, the words ending in a sob. "I hate you!"

"I hate you, too," he said in a ragged voice he barely recognized. "Now come for me again. Come for me."

Clay took a mouthful of her shoulder muscle between his teeth and bit down, grunting around her flesh as her pussy convulsed around his cock. Her entire body vibrated as she tumbled over with a wild cry, the feel of her trembling in his arms only making him wilder. Abandoning his grip on her shoulders, he clutched at her hips, squeezing tight as he rammed home again and again, driving his cock into her as she clawed the ground and her pussy continued to pulse around him, pushing him to the breaking point.

God, he was so fucking close, the precipice was looming. He knew there was something he needed to remember, but he couldn't think straight, couldn't regain control.

He was lost in her—her heat, her smell, the way her cunt clutched at his thickness, coating him in her heat—and this was the only way to get free. He came with a roar, pulsing inside her body, his balls aching and his cock jerking and a pained, tortured feeling spreading through his chest as he felt the thick jets of cum gushing inside her.

Shit. Holy shit.

Even as his body flushed with the bliss of release, misery and regret crept around from behind to sucker-punch him in the gut.

He'd come inside her. He'd fucked her bare and God only knew if she was on birth control. Considering he was pretty sure she'd told him to pull out, the answer was probably no.

What the fuck had he been thinking?

*You weren't thinking. She destroys your capacity for rational thought.*

*Admit it and take appropriate measures before you get her knocked up again and have to spend nine months with this psychopath, waiting for your second child to be born.*

The thought made his throat lock up as he pulled out of her, sitting back on his heels with a ragged sigh. She could be pregnant already. It could already be too late.

Unless…

"Get up," he said, swallowing hard as he stood, hitching his shorts up around his hips and jerking the waist tie tighter. "We're going to the infirmary."

She staggered to her feet, clutching the remains of her shirt around her as she turned to face him, tears streaming down her cheeks.

"Get your shorts." He met her angry, tear-filled eyes, willing his heart to stay locked safely inside the walls of stone he'd erected years ago, after waking up in the hospital and learning his fiancée had been killed in the car wreck that had nearly claimed his own life. "I'll find a sewing kit and you can try to fix them."

"I hate you," she whispered, making no move to reach for her shorts.

"You said that," he snapped. "It didn't keep you from coming."

Her jaw clenched. "I told you to pull out! I didn't want this."

"Are you saying I raped you?" His eyebrows drifted up his forehead.

He sounded like he couldn't care less, but inside his blood had gone cold. She had obviously been consenting at one point—hating him as much as he hated her, but consenting—but had something changed along the way? He honestly couldn't remember. It was like he'd gone out of his mind, losing every bit of the control that had made him one of the best agents in the field.

"Obviously not," she finally said, swallowing hard, as if it sickened her to say the words. "But if I'm pregnant, I will kill you. I swear I will. I won't let you anywhere near any of my children."

"There were female operatives on this base at one point," he said, forcing a bored note into his tone, even though he was so fucking relieved his knees felt weak. He hadn't crossed that line and now he had a second chance to do this right. "There might be morning-after pills in the infirmary. I suggest we go look for one because the last thing I want is to curse another one of my children with you for a mother."

Harley's eyes narrowed as she shook her head slowly from side to side. "You're the curse. I will die before I tell you where Jasper is. He's better off with no parents than ending up with a monster like you."

Clay reached down, snatching her shorts from the ground before grabbing her by the elbow. But he held her lightly. He wasn't going to lose control again. He would make sure of it, by putting Harley where he should have put her in the first place—in a cell, with steel walls to keep her in and a steel door to keep them from getting too close to each other and igniting the dirty bomb that lived between them.

"You think I'm bluffing," she said, allowing herself to be led along beside him, through the clearing and toward the main operations building beyond. "But I'm not."

"I don't think you're bluffing," he said. "I made the mistake of underestimating you. But from now on I'm going to treat you very seriously."

She glanced sharply up at him, but he didn't turn his head. He kept his gaze on the simple white and brown building ahead of him and his eyes empty, giving Harley no warning that she would be spending the rest of their time together in one of the CIA's sensory stimulation cells.

There would be no deals; there would be no easy out.

He had proven that he lacked the emotional distance to interrogate her and she had shown him that she would rather take her chances with a cobra than give him her trust. And why should she trust him? He'd proven he had no control, just like she'd proven she had no heart.

The best thing for both of them would be to let the cell do the work and keep interaction between them to a minimum.

But as he resigned himself to never touching her again, something deep inside his bones howled in protest. That animal inside didn't want to do the right thing. It wanted to pick her up, set her on the counter of the infirmary, and get back between her legs. It wanted to fuck until all the hate was gone and it could finally burst through the bars of its cage and be free.

That mindless creature insisted that sexing Harley out of his system was the only way to put the past behind him.

But that wasn't going to happen. As soon as he had taken care of her wounds, found the medicine she needed, and given her something to eat and drink, they wouldn't touch again until the day he let her out of her cell. And by that time, Jasper would already be safe at Clay's house in Maryland. He would have his son and a second chance at life waiting for him across the sea and no reason to want to waste another second with the monster who got away.

He opened the door, letting Harley precede him into the darkened facility, keeping his gaze on her shoulders instead of the bare cheeks of her ass peeking out from beneath her shirt, ignoring the stirring in his shorts as his cock insisted he wasn't finished with Harley.

Not by a long shot.

# DIRTY TWISTED LOVE

# CHAPTER ELEVEN

Marlowe

Marlowe arrived at Harley's seaside cottage three days before her sculptures were due, intending to deliver an invitation to expand their relationship in person. He had lost two of his best pilots—one to a crash over the Alps and another to a bullet between the eyes—and he needed someone he could trust to fly the next shipment into Russia.

But instead of his pretty artist with the clever hands and feline smile, he'd found empty rooms with the lights still on, a mess on the kitchen stove, and a shattered beer bottle on the patio overlooking the sea.

"There's no sign of a break-in or a struggle, sir." Liam came to stand beside him. "But I did find this."

Marlowe reached out, taking a child's drawing from his pilot's meaty hand. It was a map of the house and the surrounding areas, with a trail drawn in crayon and an X to mark the spot where the treasure was buried. It was signed by the artist—Jasper Garrett.

Marlowe smiled. "Garrett? That's her old alias."

"It is," Liam confirmed. "I told you she was hiding something."

"You did," Marlowe agreed mildly, never one to get angry with his staff for his own mistakes. "I should have listened. Any idea what might have become of her and the little one?"

"Not yet," Liam said. "Give me some

time. I should be able to turn up something. If one of our enemies took her, they'll be in touch."

"And if not, we'll figure out where our girl has gone." Marlowe handed the drawing back to Liam. "But before we go hunting, I want to see what the little man left behind."

He and Liam located shovels in the shed and followed the crudely drawn map to a hollow in the sand at the base of a grassy dune. Ten minutes later they had unearthed sand toys, a red shovel, and a damp, sand-encrusted towel. Marlowe left the towel but instructed Liam to bring the toys and the shovel.

One never knew when treasure might come in handy.

A red shovel could flatten the skull of a rival who had dared to abduct one of his associates. And a plastic bucket could be used to collect precious blood as it dripped from a little boy's throat, teaching his mother a lesson about what happened to people who tried to leave Marlowe's family.

There was no way out of the Raposa cartel,

there was only dead.

Leaving the glass on the patio and the flies circling the fishy-smelling mess on the stove, Marlowe walked through the bungalow's door to the waiting car, knowing he would find Harley sooner or later.

There was no question of if, only when.

Harley and Clay's story continues in
Filthy Wicked Love

FILTHY WICKED LOVE

**Kidnapped by the Billionaire**
**Book One**

By Lili Valente

# CHAPTER ONE

Harley

*Six Years Ago*

It was another hot, humid night in the hell that was Virginia in July. The muggy evening air had transformed Harley's blowout into a frizzy tangle, the sea breeze held the hint of dead fish swept onshore by last night's summer storm, and her legs ached from a two-mile hike along the coast with yet another man who was unhealthily obsessed with exercise.

But even sticky, sore, and fish-scented, Harley couldn't remember the last time she'd enjoyed a date this much. She felt like a normal girl on a walk with a normal guy—no darkness or head games involved.

*Normal, riiight.*

*Because normal girls always make it their mission in life to seduce their boyfriend's best friend.*

"What's so funny?" Clay's hand came to rest at the small of her back, guiding her to the side of the trail as a couple on a tandem bike raced toward them, taking up more than their fair share of the sandy strip of pavement.

"You," she lied, staying close after the couple had zipped past. This time, Clay didn't move away. He was weakening, weakening, more with every passing day. "Sleepwalking naked when you were ten years old is really your deepest, darkest secret? The *most* embarrassing thing you've done in your entire life?"

"It is." He shoved his hands into the

pockets of the cargo shorts that rode low on his hips, stretching the fabric tight, emphasizing the delicious curve of his ass.

Damn, but that thickly muscled ass was a thing of beauty.

She couldn't help sneaking peeks at it when he wasn't looking, even though she knew it wasn't time to take her seduction to the next level. Luring him into her bed certainly wasn't going to be any hardship. She wouldn't have to grit her teeth and pretend to enjoy herself the way she did with Jackson. She already knew that she and Clay would be combustible together.

All she had to do was break through the wall he'd built to keep himself from falling for his best friend's girl.

"I was traumatized for years," he continued. "I set up booby traps between my bed and the door so I would trip over something and wake up before I could strip down and make it out of my room."

She giggled.

"Are you laughing at my pain?" He shot a mock glare her way.

"I am," she said, grinning. "And I don't feel even a little bit bad about it."

Clay laughed that deep rumble that reminded her of the crunch of tires on gravel, one of her favorite sounds when she was a little girl. For a moment, she was tempted to tell him that. To tell him how she would order her driver to roll down the windows every morning on the way to school, no matter how cold the winter air, so that she could hear the tires munching the rocks on the long drive down to the road.

But she couldn't tell Clay that particular truth. To him, she was Harley Garrett, struggling cocktail waitress, not Harley Mason, artist and heiress, and that was how things had to stay, no matter how much she would like to let down her guard. She'd never been tempted like this before, but something about Clay made her want to forget the darkness that had brought her here, to forget that the sun rose with the ruins of our past mistakes glued to the horizon casting inescapable shadows.

She blinked the weak thought away. If she

wasn't careful, she would be as soft and useless as her sister by the end of the summer. "Seriously, though, you shouldn't be embarrassed of anything that happened when you were a kid. I bet you were an adorable naked sleepwalker."

"My big sister and everyone at her sweet sixteen birthday party would probably disagree," he said, grinning as he ran a hand through his closely shorn hair, the gesture so effortlessly sexy it made Harley feel flushed all over. "But I appreciate the get out of shame free card."

"Shame is a wasted emotion," she murmured, still distracted by the way he affected her, without even seeming to try.

"I agree." His hand returned to the small of her back, guiding her to the left as the trail split in two, setting her blood to pumping faster. "Remorse can be good if it inspires a change for the better, but shame poisons everything it touches."

She glanced up at him, heart lurching as their gazes connected. With his hair glowing gold in the setting sun and his blue eyes glittering with a mixture of intelligence and compassion that made him seem so much older than twenty-six, there were times when he literally took her breath away.

And she had no earthly idea why.

Harley had dated dozens of beautiful people and was currently sleeping with a marine whose body put an action hero's to shame, but none of them measured up to this golden man who shone from the inside out. She had never felt so moved, so out of control, or so disinclined to care if Clay Hart was breaking through her defenses, getting close to the walled city inside of her where no man had ever set foot.

Hell, she didn't spend much time in there herself. She preferred to ignore the last bastion of goodness left inside of her, where Innocence, Hope, and Integrity huddled behind crumbling walls, wondering when it would be their turn to be crushed beneath the weight of her sins.

"What are you thinking?" Clay's fingers curled lightly into her hip, making her acutely aware of how much she wanted him to touch her somewhere else, *everywhere* else. She wanted his light burning through the darkness, making her feel human again, making her feel something that wasn't ugly or angry or sad.

"I don't know." She fought the urge to lean into him and wrap her arms tight around his waist.

It was too soon. He was close to breaking, but he still needed more time. And he had to be the one to make the first move—or at least think that he had—for her plan to work.

But God, she wanted to touch him so badly. She wanted his taste in her mouth and his strength filling her up and his warm hands trailing over her skin, banishing the cold that seemed to follow her no matter what the season.

"Liar," he whispered, setting her heart to racing again. "Tell me."

"I've been listening to a song over and over again on the way to work," she said, the words tumbling out without her permission. "There's this one line about innocence, how it dies howling." She laughed, a soft, fearful sound that threatened to give her secrets away. "I think about it all the time. And I don't know why."

*Just like I don't know why I can't stop thinking about you.*

*Dreaming about you.*

*Waking up in the night reaching for you and wanting to cry when it's Jackson there instead.*

Clay leaned down, the light in his eyes fading as he bent his head closer to hers. "I know something's wrong, Harley. I know that something, or someone, is scaring you. I don't want to push, but if you want to talk, I'll listen and do whatever I can to help."

She swallowed hard. He was so smart, so perceptive. She had only dropped the tiniest of hints about Jackson's "abuse," not wanting to play her hand too soon, but Clay had already picked up on them.

He was making her job so easy. She should be thrilled.

Everything was ticking along right on schedule. Clay was so close to giving in to the chemistry that crackled in the air between them. Before the summer was over, she would convince him that his best friend was a monster who beat and terrorized her. And then Clay would have permission to stop thinking with his honorable heart and start thinking with his dick, like every other man on earth, and he would be putty in her hands.

He was practically conning himself, but for some reason, the worry in his eyes didn't make her want to rush home and break out the champagne. It made her want to cry, to press her face against his chest and confess all the dirty secrets she was keeping.

She had never believed in religion or divine forgiveness, but she believed in Clay. If someone so good could care about her, forgive her, then maybe she wasn't beyond redemption after all.

"Don't cry," he whispered, his big hand coming to cup her cheek. "I can't stand to see you cry."

She blinked away her tears, willing herself to get a fucking grip. This wasn't the time for the big breakdown. She had to stick to the plan and make sure she had bruises to back up her claims before she pulled the trigger on phase two.

"It's nothing." She stepped back, putting some much-needed distance between them. "I've just been working too much, pulling too many late nights in a row." She shrugged, the ghost of a smile flickering across her face before it vanished, evaporating into the muggy air. "Makes me a little morbid, I guess."

"Are you sure that's all?" he pressed. "You can tell me anything, Harley. I hope you know that. I'm not the kind of person who runs when things get hard."

"I know," she said because she did.

She'd only met Clay a month ago, but he'd already proven that he was braver than any man she'd ever known. He was a decorated marine, who had been awarded the Purple Heart when he was wounded saving another soldier's life, but it wasn't his military prowess that impressed her. It was the way he knew himself, inside and out. Only a person who had looked long and hard at the deepest, darkest parts of his own soul could know his heart that well.

Most mornings, Harley was terrified of her own reflection. She would never have Clay's courage or even Jackson's. At least Jackson knew what he wanted, even if he was too stupid to see that she hated every minute she spent pretending to enjoy his bossy bullshit in the bedroom.

Harley had no idea what she wanted, not really.

She was doing her best to take revenge against the man who had ruined her mother because she had been taught to ruthlessly and efficiently punish her enemies. It was one of the ways she prepared herself to take her place as head of the Mason family. Her sister Hannah was too weak, too sweet, and too forgiving to fill their father's shoes. A rough, cruel world required a cold, heartless captain at the helm. Harley was that captain and she had never hesitated to make the sacrifices necessary to ensure that she remained at the top of the food chain.

But maybe there was more to life than dominance and control.

Maybe there was something to be said for

kindness, for gentleness, for…love.

Her heart rustled uncomfortably in her chest.

*Love.*

She knew what it felt like—she loved her sister and her mother, too, even if it had been years since Emma Mason had looked at her with anything but pain and regret in her eyes—but Harley had never expected to feel that particular emotion for a man. Men were to be used for pleasure, gain, or influence and discarded when they were no longer useful. Men were easily led, but not so easily ruled and should never be trusted with important, breakable things like hearts or souls, hopes or dreams.

Harley didn't even love her own father. She admired him, aspired to be like him, wanted to please him, but she didn't love him. She'd realized at a young age that Stewart would never love her back and even as a child Harley had been too practical to waste her time or energy on lost causes.

But Clay wasn't a lost cause, and when she was with him, she could almost believe that she wasn't either.

She tilted her head back, the mixture of worry, hope, and confusion in his expression assuring her it was time to readjust her plans. Clay was already in the palm of her hand. She had never expected to fall in love with him, but now that she had, it was easy to see the same emotion reflected in his deep blue eyes. He loved her, he truly did, and for once, the thought of a man loving her didn't make her want to run away.

"I'm in love with someone," she said, her voice trembling with very real emotion. "But I'll never be able to be with him."

"Why?" Clay asked, his voice soft.

"Because Jackson is never going to let me go. At least not in one piece," she whispered, the flash of recognition in Clay's eyes assuring her she wasn't jumping the gun.

He had been expecting to hear something like this. Now all she had to do was give him the last piece of the puzzle and he would be hers.

She stepped closer, until his warmth caressed the front of her body and his evergreen and soap smell filled her head. "Especially not if I tell him that it… That it's you."

Pain and relief flashed across Clay's features. "Jesus, Harley."

"I'm sorry." She pressed her lips together, pretending she didn't understand that he was already in too deep to get away from her now. "I know you can't possibly feel the same way. I know you and Jackson have been friends for forever, but I can't—"

"Stop." Clay's arms went around her waist, pulling her against him, sending an electric shock of awareness dancing across her skin.

She had never been this close to him and it was every bit as delicious as she'd imagined it would be. Her nipples pulled tight inside her bra, aching to be skin to skin with this man, to know what it was like to make love to someone who was so completely beautiful, inside and out.

"I do feel the same way," he said, his voice rough with emotion. "I've been trying to deny it, but you're all I think about, all I dream about. And every time we say goodbye, I'm fucking miserable until I see you again."

"Me too," she said, lips tingling as she tilted her head back. "I want to kiss you so badly it hurts."

"I'll never hurt you," Clay said, bending his head closer to hers. "And I won't let him hurt you, either. I won't let anyone hurt you ever again."

Their lips met and fireworks exploded behind Harley's eyes. Her head spun and her cells ignited with an inferno of need that made every other lustful moment of her life pale in comparison. His arms tightened around her, lifting her off the ground as his tongue swept through her mouth, stroking against hers.

By the time his hands drifted down to her bottom, molding her flesh in his palms as their kiss grew wild, almost frantic, she knew she wouldn't be going home alone. By the time he slammed the door to her apartment behind him and rolled her beneath him on the carpet just inside the door—they were both too desperate for each other to make it to the bedroom—she knew she would never feel this way about another man.

As their clothes vanished and their mouths met again and Clay slid inside her, fucking her slow and deep while he whispered sweet things that were also true things because he was a man in love, Harley forgot that this was part of a bigger, uglier agenda. For a few blissful moments, she was simply a woman making love to a man, falling apart in Clay's arms and coming back together with a piece of him locked away inside her heart.

And that piece of him stayed alive inside of her for years.

Until the day that love turned to hate and her heart grew edges sharp enough to cut its way free from her flesh and bone.

# CHAPTER TWO

Harley

*Present Day*

*Stop. Please stop, please stop, please stop...*
Harley curled into a ball on her side on the hard cot, covering her head with her pillow and smashing her hands down on top. But the song was still there, droning faintly on and on, endlessly repeating,

unraveling her sanity a little more each time it ended only to start all over again.

*Sexy as the devil and twice as sweet, innocence died howling my name.*

*Howling, howling, never the same...*

The lyrics taunted her, wrapping around her head and squeezing until she whimpered.

She wasn't going to die howling. She didn't have the strength left to howl.

She had no idea how long she'd been in this torture chamber, but it had to have been at least a week. She'd started her period the day after she was locked away—thank God for his ugly little favors—and bled for the usual three days. After that, she had tried counting the meal trays to keep up with the passage of time but had lost track after the fifth tray shoved through the slot in the door.

But there had been more trays after that. A lot more. Simple, but perfectly acceptable meals that she'd left mostly untouched. Not because she was deliberately trying to starve herself; her body was simply too fucked up to recognize hunger or exhaustion or much of anything else.

The torment had started slowly at first—hours of it being slightly too cold in the cell, followed by hours of it being slightly too hot. She'd dealt with the extremes by taking too-frequent showers in the tiny stall near the toilet in the corner of her cell, warming up in the hot spray or cooling down with a lukewarm mist she allowed to air dry on her skin. But gradually the hot and cold had grown more extreme until she was vacillating between shivering and sweating and the temperature contrasts could no longer be explained away by an antiquated cooling system.

She'd realized that Clay was deliberately manipulating the conditions in the cell to torture her into giving him what he wanted and gone to bed that night sweating furiously, her rage burning as fiery as the heat in the room.

The suffering continued on day two when hot and cold were replaced by light and dark. Not long after her breakfast tray was delivered the lights abruptly shut off, plunging her into blackness that stretched on for far longer than an average night—or at least she suspected it had. She had no way to track the passing hours, but by the time the lights finally flickered back on, stinging her widely dilated pupils, she had been silently praying for an end to the darkness for what felt like an eternity.

But she hadn't said a word aloud, hadn't made the slightest sound. Her lips remained closed and her features as impassive as she could make them. She refused to grant Clay the satisfaction of knowing how miserable he was making her or give him any hope that his methods were going to succeed.

He never visited her in her cell or spoke when he slipped her meal trays and other supplies through the slot in the door, but there were cameras on the ceiling. She knew he was watching, listening, waiting for her to break. But she wouldn't betray her son. She would die before she helped Clay find him.

If she couldn't be there for Jasper, the very least she could do was spare him the torture of being raised by a madman.

As the days stretched on, Harley withdrew

from the outside world, divorcing herself from her suffering, confused body as much as possible. In the happier corners of her mind, she relived beautiful moments with Jasper, long summer days with Hannah, and any other sweet memory she could hold onto long enough to get lost inside of it. She was holding together fairly well—especially considering how messed up she'd been when Clay had tossed her into the cell, still bruised and aching and hating herself for fucking a man who'd nearly killed her—until The Day the Music Died.

"The day the music died," Harley muttered softly, beneath her pillow.

No, the music wasn't dying. Something inside of her was dying, being slowly eroded by a beautiful thing put to an ugly purpose.

She'd never imagined music could be used as a weapon, but this…

*Sexy as the devil and twice as sweet, twice as sweet…*

It was horrible, worms crawling into her ears and squirming through her brain, making her wish she could stab holes in her eardrums.

*Innocence died howling, howling my name...*

If only he would play something else, anything else, just for a few minutes, maybe she would be able to pull her shit together. But it was only this song—the one she'd once told him haunted her—over and over again. Sometimes played so softly it was like mice gnawing away inside the walls, making her itch in unreachable places, sometimes so loud it made her head throb as she prowled back and forth in her cell, fighting to keep from hurling her body against the door and screaming for Clay to come let her out.

But she wouldn't scream. She wouldn't give him the satisfaction.

No more satisfaction for him. No. Fucking. More.

She'd sworn that to herself when she'd forced that morning-after pill down her bruised throat, hating herself for needing one.

But she hadn't been able to control herself. Even as every spark of love she'd felt for Clay had transformed into hate so sharp it sliced at the sensitive places inside of her, she still craved his hands on her, his taste in her mouth, his cock working between her legs, fucking her until she fell to pieces. She'd always heard that love and hate were better friends than most people realized, but now she knew it with a certainty that thrummed through what was left of her mind.

Even as she plotted painful, terrifying ways for Clay to die—infected with some exotic disease and left to rot on this island alone, tied to the same cot she'd been bound to and slowly carved to pieces with the rusty knife she'd found in the drawer—her mind drifted to those moments when he'd brought her back to life.

That's what it had felt like, being brought back to life after centuries of numb, dreamless sleep.

But Sleeping Beauty hadn't been awakened by a kiss.

She had been awakened by cruel hands squeezing her breasts, hateful words whispered in her ear, and fingers curling roughly inside her, forcing her into an orgasm she hadn't wanted to give. The pleasure had come from cruelty and should have been repulsive. But she'd been waiting so long to feel something with her entire self, waiting so long for the frozen place inside her to thaw, that she had relished every ugly, beautiful second of the bliss Clay had given her and come so hard she'd seen stars.

It was sick, but even after these long, miserable days as his prisoner, if he came into the cell and slipped his hand up the white tee shirt he'd given her to wear and cupped her breast in his warm, rough hand, she knew she would fuck him again. She would bite and scratch and bleed another orgasm from his body just for the pleasure of watching his face twist as he tumbled over, proving she wasn't the only one powerless against the chemistry that seethed between them, ready to explode at the slightest provocation.

As she lay on her cot, listening to the singer's smoky voice keen about killing every sweet thing he touched, she couldn't keep her thoughts from drifting to that moment when Clay had pinned her beneath him. Her skin flushed hot beneath the covers as she recalled the exact moment she'd realized that he was going to fuck her on the ground, like an animal, the rush of shock and lust that had sent her blood rocketing through her veins.

If she concentrated, she could almost feel the dull pain of his teeth biting into the muscled flesh on her shoulder and the rush of heat between her legs as her body responded to the hunger he awakened within her. She had wanted it, wanted *him*. Even as she'd cursed him, she'd relished the feel of his thick cock tunneling into her, demanding that she take every inch of him. He'd fucked her with complete possession, staking a claim on her body that some primitive part of her had responded to with abandon.

Just thinking about it was enough to make her nipples tighten and the crotch of the boxers she wore—Clay's; he had torn her own clothes to shreds—grow damp. She longed to slip her hand below the too big waistband of the boxers and find her clit, to slide her fingers through her slick folds, bringing herself to completion while she imagined Clay's cock inside her, his mouth hot on her nipples as he licked and sucked her sensitive flesh.

But she couldn't. He was watching.

There were two fish-eye cameras in the corners of the room that took in the entire space. If she touched herself, Clay would see and know that she was weak, needy, desperate for something to take her mind off the torture of these four walls and the misery he was inflicting.

*Sank into you soft and deep. Innocence died howling my name…*

She rolled onto her back and stared up at the ceiling, letting the song grate against her already raw nerves, hoping it would banish the lust heating her skin. But her nipples only pebbled tighter, poking through the thin fabric of her shirt. She closed her eyes and bit down hard on the inside of her lip, fighting the urge to shift her thighs, willing herself to think of anything else.

She tried thinking of Marlowe and what would happen if his people got to her house before she did and discovered the evidence of Jasper's existence that she hadn't had the chance to erase. She was scheduled to have shipped the drugs last Friday. When the sculptures hadn't reached their destinations by Wednesday or Thursday—which could be any day now—Marlowe would send a team to her bungalow on the beach.

He might even come himself. She'd never missed a shipment and Marlowe would be worried about her safety. He would never suspect that she'd crossed him, a fact she'd counted on when she'd planned to fake her own death. But now that plan had gone to shit, and if she didn't do something soon, Marlowe would realize that she'd been hiding her son from him for years.

Even a day ago, that knowledge had been enough to clear her thoughts of anything but the need for escape. But that was before a song had carried her down to hell and made her twist there.

Now, she couldn't hold on to logical thought long enough for it to have any power over her. Now, she was weakening, weakening…

*Innocence died howling…*
*Howling my name…*

She wasn't innocent, hadn't been since she was thirteen years old and getting fingered by college boys behind the canoe rentals as the summer wound to a close and the last of her childhood went up in flames.

And she didn't want to die howling or any other way.

She wanted to live, but she couldn't survive another day in this chamber of horrors without something to ease the pain. She needed relief, respite, just a few moments of pleasure to remind her that there was a world beyond the hell Clay had created just for her.

Closing her eyes, Harley let her walls crumble and the brutal fantasy come rushing in.

# CHAPTER THREE

## Harley

With a moan of surrender, Harley's hands drifted up to cup her breasts through the tee shirt fabric. She captured her nipples and rolled them in slow circles, tightening her grip until it stung, until it felt like the way *he'd* touched her, that son of a bitch.

She hated him.

She would gladly walk over his dead body if it were the only way out of this cell, but she still wanted him, too. She wanted him hard and ugly and fierce, both of them surrendering to lust and contempt in equal measure.

Her hate and her lust fed on each other, like fire and kindling, burning hotter until her nerves crackled with electricity. Her breath grew faster and her thighs grew damp, but she continued to torment her nipples, building the need swelling inside of her until the music faded away and all she could hear was the blood rushing in her ears and her body crying out for release.

Until she could imagine it was Clay's fingers pinching and tugging at her sensitive flesh, Clay's hand smoothing down her fluttering belly, Clay's voice rough in her ear as he worked her closer to the edge.

*"This is what you want." His fingers drove between her legs, shoving in and up, hitting that place deep inside of her that made her cry out. "You want me to fuck you until you can't remember your own name. Until you forget that you were ever anything but*

*my whore."*

*"I'm not your whore,"* she said, lifting into his hand in spite of herself. His touch just felt so fucking good, so bad, so the opposite of long numb days spent staring at the same bare walls. *"Whores get paid, asshole."*

*"You'll get paid."* He ripped her boxers down her legs before spreading her wide, his thumbs digging into her thighs as he bared her shamefully wet pussy. *"Give me what I want and I'll let you go."*

*"I don't believe you,"* she said, her words ending in a shudder as he settled between her thighs, trapping his rigid cock between their bodies.

Fuck. He was so hard and hot and she wanted him so much. She wanted his tongue fucking her mouth and his teeth bruising her flesh and his cock stroking between her legs, making her come so hard it felt like her cells were in the midst of a nuclear reaction.

She arched her back, pressing her breasts tighter to his chest as she squirmed her hips, trying to fit their bodies together.

*"It doesn't matter if you believe me."* His breath was warm on her neck as he rocked his hips, just once, making her moan as his hardness rubbed against her

*clit. "What you think, what you feel, what you want—none of it matters. All that matters is that you tell me what I need to know. Give in, Harley. Make it easy on both of us."*

*She bit down on her lip until she tasted blood, fighting the urge to grind against him, but it was so hard. She craved friction, movement, and the stretch of her inner walls as Clay rammed inside of her. She'd been with men who were longer, but never anyone thicker than Clay. Even when she'd been dripping wet and he was trying to be gentle, there had been times when they'd been a tight fit, when it had hurt for those first few strokes until her body adjusted to his girth.*

*Now, as he positioned himself and pressed just the thick head of his cock inside her, a gasp escaped her lips without her permission. He was so big, so swollen, dipping in and out of her entrance until the sting of the initial penetration became a hunger for more.*

*She lifted her hips, trying to force him deeper, but he captured them in his big hands, pinning her to the mattress.*

*"This is all you get." He rocked his hips, slow and shallow, making her breath come faster and her neglected clit buzz with the need for stimulation. "If you want more, you know what you need to do. Tell*

*me where Jasper is."*

*"I'm not telling you shit," she ground out. "You'll give in and fuck me, sooner or later. You want this as much as I do."*

*"You're right," he said, grunting softly as he continued his torment. "I do want you. But I can get what I need without you getting off." His hands came to her nipples, pinching them in time to his too-shallow thrusts, driving her even further out of her mind. "I can make sure you never come again if I want to. All I have to do is tie your hands and legs to the bed and watch you squirm."*

*"Stop," she begged, even as she lifted into his thrusts, taking advantage of the fact that his hands were busy elsewhere. His cock slid deeper, but still not deep enough, not nearly deep enough. She needed all of him, every inch of his thickness pounding between her legs.*

*"Stop?" He pulled out, summoning a ragged cry of protest from her lips.*

*"No! Please. Don't stop."*

*"Which is it? Stop or don't stop?" His hand dropped to his cock, tugging the swollen length with rough strokes of his hand.*

*"Don't stop," she panted, her fingers fisting in the*

*sweat-damp sheets, refusing to let herself reach for him. "Fuck me, you piece of shit."*

*"If you want me to fuck you, you know what to do," he said, batting her hand away when she tried to reach down and take care of herself, his own rhythm never faltering as he jerked himself closer to the edge. "Tell me where Jasper is."*

*"No!" Her thighs writhed on either side of his hips, the tension inside of her swelling bigger, bigger until her pelvis was flooded with heat. She was close, so fucking close despite his refusal to give her what she needed.*

*She was about to come, about to tumble over the edge screaming.*

*All she needed was one touch, light fingers between her legs or the tip of his cock brushing against her clit, and she would explode. She was almost there, almost there, so close she could—*

"Get up." The harsh voice crackling through the speakers startled her, shocking her back to the world of her cell and the reality of her own fingers driving in and out of her dripping pussy.

She pulled her hand swiftly from between her legs, shame at being caught washing through her even as another part of her delighted in the silence that filled the room.

The song was gone.

The song was gone and she was immediately stronger. Strong enough to smile as she realized that she'd finally gotten a reaction from her captor. Clay had broken his silence and the reason why was abundantly clear. She had the upper hand for the first time in God only knew how long and she intended to make use of it.

"Just a second," she said, letting her hand slide back beneath the waistband of the boxers as her other hand pushed her shirt up, baring her breast.

She moaned as her head fell back and her fingers resumed their work between her legs and at her sensitized nipple. "This won't take long. Oh my God, right there. Just like that. I'm so close, so wet."

There was no response, but Harley didn't let that stop her. She knew Clay was watching, listening, wanting. If she could get him thinking with his cock long enough to open the door to the cell, she might have another chance to escape.

"Don't you wish you were here," she said, wiggling the boxers lower on her hips, giving him a better view of her fingers teasing at her swollen clit. "I'm so ready. You could be balls deep in a few seconds, you son of a bitch."

She closed her eyes, imagining him in front of a monitor, watching her touch herself and losing the battle against coming to join her. His cock would be hard, hot, straining the zipper of his pants and his balls aching with the need for release. Or maybe he would already have his cock in hand, jerking himself while he watched her writhe on her cot, quickly realizing that fucking his own hand wasn't going to be enough.

"I hate you." She transferred her attention to her other breast. "But I want you again. I want to fuck you until we're both bruised. I want you to take me so hard I won't be able to walk tomorrow. Wouldn't you like that, baby? To fuck me that hard?"

Harley's fingers moved faster between her legs, even as her orgasm moved out of reach. She wanted Clay to think she was on the verge of coming, to believe she was incapable of making any sudden movements.

And then the second he opened that door, she would be up and out.

She moaned and arched her back, panting as she plucked harder at her nipple, putting on a good show as she slit her eyes and checked the position of her untouched lunch tray. It was still right beside the door. It didn't weigh much, but if she brought it down on Clay's head with all her strength, it might be enough to disorient him long enough for her to shut the door, locking him inside his own prison.

And then she would leave him here. Leave him to starve to death while she made her way back to Jasper.

The thought was so sweet that her womb tightened again, but she pushed the sensation away. She needed release of a different kind right now, and Clay was about to give it to her.

She heard footsteps outside the door and then soft beeping as he punched numbers into the pad on the door. She fought to keep up her pretense until the perfect moment.

She bit her lip, plunging her fingers in and out of her dripping channel as her muscles tensed, preparing to run like hell the second she saw a glimpse of the outside world.

In three, two…

# CHAPTER FOUR

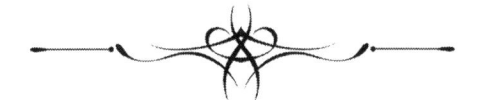

### Clay

Clay's cock had been hard as a fucking rock the moment Harley slipped her hands up to cup her breasts through her tee shirt, but she was a fool if she thought it would be this easy to get him to drop his guard.

He wasn't a goddamned teenager at the mercy of his own hormones and he'd already lost too much time.

They'd been on the island two weeks. He was burning through his two-month sabbatical far too quickly for comfort. Meanwhile, Harley had lost five pounds she couldn't afford to lose, and he was no closer to finding out where Jasper was than when they'd started. He'd seen terrorists break faster than this, under very similar sensory exhaustion techniques. It was time to stop fucking around and prove to this stubborn bitch that there would be no escape until she gave him what he needed.

Taser in hand, Clay opened the cell door and stepped inside, his lips twisting in a hard smile as Harley vaulted off the bed and sprinted toward him.

She made it three steps before he fired. The probes connected with her chest and she went rigid as she rocked back on her heels, her body toppling toward the floor. But as she fell, her right arm swept up and out, severing the current. She hit the ground and was back on her feet a second later, dodging around him to the right and lunging for the door.

Even as he grabbed her from behind, pinning her arms to her body and spinning them both back inside the cell, a spark of admiration flickered to life inside of him. No matter how crazy she made him, her will power was completely fucking impressive.

"Where did you learn that?" he asked, grunting as she thrashed in his arms, her heel connecting with his shin with enough force to bruise.

"Let me go," she snarled, writhing like a serpent, getting closer to squirming free than he would like to admit.

She hadn't been eating much, but she had been steadily increasing the number of push-ups and sit-ups she completed every few hours. At this rate, she was going to leave her cell in better shape than when she went in.

He tossed her back onto the cot. "Seriously, I want to know where you learned to overpower fifty thousand volts of electricity."

"Mind over matter," she said, her eyes darting between him and the open cell door behind him. "I meditate. A lot. You should try it. Maybe then you wouldn't be such a psychopath."

"Takes one to know one."

Her lips peeled away from her teeth. "I hope you shit yourself to death."

Unexpectedly, laughter rose in his chest, but he smothered it with a rough clearing of his throat.

"Noted." He tensed, ready to lunge for her if she made another break for the door, but she only hugged her knees to her chest and glared up at him, apparently realizing that escape wasn't going to happen today.

But who knew about tomorrow?

If she could retain her sanity for two weeks of sensory deprivation and overload and shrug off a law enforcement grade Taser like she was swatting flies, who knew what else she was capable of. They might still be here six weeks from now when his leave ran out.

At the conclusion of his sabbatical, Clay was set to rejoin the task force taking down Marlowe Reynolds. No matter how little he cared about his job these days—living in the shadows had started to lose its appeal around the same time he'd learned that he had a son and something worth living for—Clay wanted to remain a part of that operation.

Marlowe was a disease set loose upon the earth. From the day Clay had walked into a warehouse in Rome and seen ten men hanging upside down from the fifty-foot ceiling, their intestines spilling out to form ropes of gore that trailed to the dirt below, he'd promised himself he would see Marlowe behind bars. He didn't want to retire before that happened, and he didn't want to raise his son in a world with Marlowe loose in it.

Especially considering there was a chance Marlowe might decide Jasper fell under his "protection."

Reynolds had very firm opinions on family. Once someone signed on with the Raposa cartel, they were a part of that family and owed Marlowe complete loyalty for the rest of their lives. In exchange, he made sure anyone who threatened them or theirs was dealt with swiftly and efficiently.

Clay didn't want to wake up one night to find Marlowe standing over his bed, ready to exact retribution for taking Harley's son away from her. Even if she had been telling the truth about concealing Jasper's existence from her boss in the past, he didn't put it past her to send Marlowe to fetch Jasper back into the fold. Considering how she felt about Clay, she might very well decide Jasper was better off with a drug lord for a father figure.

*That's why you have to make sure Marlowe goes down and Harley believes she'll end up behind bars if she ever so much as sets foot on U.S. soil, let alone tries to contact Jasper.*

Yes, that's exactly what he had to do. Thank you, inner voice.

But neither of those fucking things was going to happen until he knew where Jasper was.

"Tell me where you sent Jasper and this ends now," he said, but he could hear the hopelessness in his own voice. She wasn't going to tell him, at least not now, so soon after getting a reaction out of him for the first time in weeks.

"Sure." She smiled. "Right after you cut off your balls and shove them up your ass."

Clay arched a wry brow. "I don't remember you having such a filthy mouth."

"Well, I didn't hate your guts the last time I knew you." She hugged her knees closer to her chest, her smile transforming into a sneer. "Loathing brings out the crasser side of my nature."

*But you still want to fuck me.*

That hadn't been a lie. He'd heard the truth in her words, in the hunger in her voice. She wanted more.

He wanted more, too. His dreams for the past two weeks had been nothing but non-stop filth. He'd had Dream Harley every dirty way he'd ever imagined fucking a woman, and a few twisted ways his subconscious had coughed up in the dead of the night, and woke up each morning sporting wood for a woman he hated. Aside from Jasper, wanting to get naked and fuck the hell out of each other was the only thing he and Harley had in common.

*And Marlowe.*

*Between the three of those things, you should be able to get what you need from her.*

*Play to your common ground and show you've got the negotiating skills of a new hire, for God's sake.*

"Get up," he said, motioning toward the door. "We're going to go for a walk."

Her eyebrows lifted. "A walk."

"I found socks and shoes for you in one of the storage rooms. We can grab those and my canteen on our way out."

"Where are we walking?" she asked, toes curling into the sheets. "And why?"

"The shoes might be a little big, but it will be better than going barefoot," he continued, ignoring her questions.

He wasn't sure where they were going just yet, but the why would soon be apparent.

Sensory deprivation hadn't gotten the job done. It was time to see what a little good old-fashioned exhaustion could do. He would walk Harley until she dropped and then he would remind her of all the things they had in common, all the ways he could make her life better if she agreed to play by his rules.

He hadn't intended to touch her again, but if it took intimate contact to chip away at her resistance, it was a sacrifice he and his raging erection were willing to make.

# FILTHY WICKED LOVE

# CHAPTER FIVE

Harley

The outside world was a revelation.

Harley had never been so grateful to feel a breeze stirring her hair or the sun on her skin. She didn't even care that she was likely going to burn without sunscreen if they were out for longer than an hour or two. All she wanted to do was lie down in the grass, spread her arms and legs like a starfish, suck the sea air deep into her lungs, and soak in the healing power of sunshine—the opposite of the glaring fluorescents that had sucked the life out of her inside her cell.

Instead, she marched sedately along in front of Clay, keeping her expression neutral and her joy at being let out of her cage to herself. She would not share her emotions with him, she would not show weakness or vulnerability, and she would not give any sign that she was ready to run at the first sign of a break in his focus.

Though he undoubtedly knew that. He'd come into her cell with a Taser, for God's sake. He still had the weapon in hand and aimed between her shoulder blades, obviously having realized that she wouldn't be able to sever the current's connection if he shot her from behind.

She couldn't believe she'd overcome the nervous system overload the first time around. She'd just been so angry and so focused on getting out and getting to Jasper that somehow she'd convinced her arm to move.

Time was growing short.

Marlowe's men would be showing up at her bungalow by the beach soon. She had to make sure she had safely disposed of every trace of Jasper's existence before they arrived. Even if she couldn't have the sculptures ready, at the very least, she had to make sure there was nothing left at the house to lead them to her son.

Considering Clay seemed determined to keep her here indefinitely, it looked like there was only one way that was going to happen.

"You have to go back to my house on Ko Tao," she said as they started down the dirt trail leading into the rainforest. "I was supposed to ship my next batch of statues last Friday. If they don't arrive at their destinations by the tenth, Marlowe will send a team to find out why. You have to make sure Jasper's room is empty and all signs that he was ever at the house are gone before they get there."

"So you really have kept Jasper a secret," Clay said, his voice as calm and unmoved as it had been since the moment he appeared in her cell.

If she hadn't seen the telltale bulge at the front of his shorts, she would have believed he'd been indifferent to her little show.

But she had seen it. He still wanted her and she intended to use that weakness against him at the first opportunity. She just had to make sure she kept her own weakness for him under lock and key. Focusing on Jasper was the best way to do that.

"Yes. I told you, nothing is more important to me than Jasper. His safety and happiness are my first priority."

Clay grunted softly. "If that were true, you would have warned me that I needed to take care of clean up before now. At this point, there's no way I could get to your house before Marlowe's people. It's already the sixteenth."

Harley spun to face him, staggering to a stop in the middle of the trail as her blood ran cold. "What?"

"Today is June sixteenth," he repeated, his eyes flat, unreadable. "You were in the cell for two weeks."

Her jaw dropped.

She couldn't help herself. She had estimated a week at the very most.

*No.* She shook her head slowly back and forth. There was no way she'd lost two weeks of her life. It couldn't have been that long.

"You're lying," she said, fresh anger surging hotly inside her chest. "You're lying to get me to tell you where Jasper is."

"I'm not lying. See for yourself." He reached for the strap of his watch. When it slipped free, he tossed it to her, keeping the stun gun aimed at her chest as he moved.

She caught the black band and twisted it in her fingers, glancing down to see the display insisting it was ten fifteen in the morning on June sixteenth.

Her mouth went dry, terror and rage fighting for supremacy. "You could have rigged this," she said, but the accusation sounded far-fetched, even to her own ears.

"I could have, but I didn't." He shifted closer. "Which means that Marlowe either already knows that you're missing or he will know very soon. And he will also know that you have a son you've been hiding from him."

He paused, giving that miserable knowledge a moment to sink in.

As if she needed it. She'd had nightmares about Marlowe discovering Jasper's existence for years.

"Understanding Marlowe the way I do," he continued in that infuriatingly calm voice, "I'm sure he'll begin searching for both of you immediately. You're going to be hard to find. Jasper…" His head tilted to one side and then the other. "Maybe not so hard, not for someone with the web of connections your boss has."

Harley swallowed, forcing her saliva down her throat. The muscles there had stopped hurting several days ago—maybe a week ago, she realized, her head spinning as the time she'd lost hit her all over again—but the flesh suddenly felt bruised again.

She had fucked up. Clay was right. She should have told him about the need for cleanup sooner. Maybe he would have listened. He seemed to want Jasper safe, even if he was going about it all wrong.

"It's okay," he said, his voice gentler than it had been since they arrived on the island. "You held up better in there than anyone I've ever seen, but the cell fucks with your head. It's no wonder you weren't thinking straight."

Her eyes squeezed shut. His kindness hurt more than his anger, but he probably knew that, too.

He was clearly no newbie to any of this sick, twisted shit.

"What are you?" She forced her eyes open, fighting the panic and fear swelling inside her. "The DEA doesn't have secret prisons in the middle of the Gulf of Thailand. And not even the FBI is this fucked up. So I'm guessing, what—CIA?"

He inclined his head. It wasn't an answer, but it was close enough.

So he was CIA. Or at least he used to be. She couldn't imagine even the CIA condoning an agent kidnapping and imprisoning his former fiancée. And if they had, they would want information on Marlowe, not Jasper.

"But they don't know you're here," she

said, crossing her arms at her chest. "Have you gone rogue, Clay? That's what they call it, right? When an operative cracks and goes off the rails."

"Why would you think that?" he asked, his lips curving.

"If you weren't off the rails, we wouldn't be the only ones on the island, and the furniture in the cottage and the counters in the pharmacy wouldn't have been covered with dust," she said, determined to banish his cocky grin. "You're here without permission, using a government facility to carry out a personal vendetta. If your superiors or your former boss or whoever finds out, I can't imagine that will go well for you."

"You're part of a case I've been working on for a long time," he said, his voice still calm. "And I have the liberty to carry out investigations the way I see fit."

His smile soured at the edges. "It's ironic really. I've been close to learning you were alive for so many years. Even if I hadn't been keeping an eye on Jackson and he hadn't found your sister, our paths would have crossed sooner or later. Probably sooner now that my team is closing in on the cartel."

"Guess we were meant to be," Harley said through gritted teeth.

"All of Marlowe's people will be spending the rest of their lives in prison," he said, his gaze shifting pointedly over her shoulder, toward the main building and the cell he'd used to torture her. "All that remains to be seen is if you'll end up in a place like this or back in the States where you'll have access to a lawyer and at least a shot in hell of seeing freedom before you're too old to enjoy it."

She narrowed her eyes, searching his face. "Were you always this good at lying? Was I just too naïve to see it when we were younger?"

"Naïve isn't a word I would use to describe you at any age," he said dryly. "And I'm not lying."

He paused, something she couldn't read flickering in his eyes. "But I do feel bad for what happened between us that first day. That was never part of the plan. And you're right, my superiors wouldn't be happy to learn I fucked a woman I'm supposed to be interrogating."

He let the Taser drop slowly to his side. "Because of that, I'm willing to offer you a deal."

A deal. Another deal with another devil.

She was never going to escape them. She was doomed to spend her life passing out of one fire and into the next, descending through the levels of hell, meeting the men who were its masters.

Looking at Clay now, seeing the sunlight filtering through the trees catching his sandy blond hair, transforming it into a golden halo, she wondered if maybe she'd finally found rock bottom.

Lucifer, the king of hell, the prince of lies, was supposed to be beautiful, wasn't he? Like Clay?

Beautiful and smooth and seductive until the moment he betrayed you to the death and worse. It was the beauty that made the betrayal truly heinous, which made it so exquisitely terrible when he took your hand and led you into the fire.

# CHAPTER SIX

### Harley

"A deal." Harley forced a smile, already knowing she didn't want anything he had to offer. "What kind of a deal?"

He was lying. She could feel it in her gut, no matter how solid his poker face. He was here without permission and any promises he made weren't worth the paper they were written on.

"The best thing we can do for Jasper is to make sure Marlowe never finds him," Clay said, his voice thick with worry. "We need him to disappear and I can make that happen. I have the connections to change his name, his appearance, and erase all connections to Marlowe or anyone else who might want to hurt him. I can keep him safe and give him a chance at a normal life."

A normal life.

Even knowing Clay was incapable of delivering on that promise—Marlowe wasn't so easily escaped—the phrase still sent a sharp pang through her chest. It was all she wanted for Jasper, all she'd ever wanted.

Clay eased closer, sending the familiar smell of him sweeping through her head. "All you have to do is tell me where he is."

"And in exchange?" she asked, fighting to hide her hurt and anger. He had mentioned a deal and she was curious what Clay assumed was a fair price for handing her child over to a man who had nearly killed her.

"In exchange, I destroy the file I have on

you." Hope flickered in his eyes, there and gone in a second, but long enough for Harley to see how much he wanted this to be over. She might have been the one in the cell, but Clay hadn't enjoyed torturing her. Apparently he hadn't become a complete sadist in the years that they'd been apart.

Someone should give him a medal.

A big, heavy one, swung straight into his handsome face.

"I haven't shared what I have on you with anyone else in the agency," he continued. "It can go directly into the trash and you can go free. I can even help you find a place to hide until Marlowe is in custody and it's safe for you to show your face again."

"Safe for me to come see Jasper," she said, arching a cool brow. "And help give him a normal childhood."

Clay's jaw tightened. "We can never be sure that we've captured all of Marlowe's associates. His network is too wide. I know it will be painful for you, but the best thing for Jasper is to let him go."

She kept her breath long and smooth,

refusing to shout or let this devolve into a rage fest the way it had the first time he'd told her that she would never see her son again. This time, she would use logic, appeal to the compassion he felt for his son, and hope that Clay had cooled down enough to listen to what she had to say.

He didn't seem as angry as he had that first day on the island. Maybe the two weeks she'd lost would be worth something, after all, if they gave her a shot at making him see reason.

"I told my share of lies when we were together," she said, keeping her tone even, reasonable. "But I wasn't lying about my mother. She abandoned our family when I was ten years old. One day she was there helping with homework and teaching my sister and me to cook from this old French cookbook and the next day she was just…gone. Even knowing that she'd left of her own free will didn't keep me from loving her, needing her, and praying every day that she would come home and be my mother again."

Clay's lids dropped to half-mast. "That

must have been hard."

"And then she came back," Harley pressed on, needing him to know the whole story, to see the bigger picture. "But she wasn't the same. She didn't want to look at me, let alone teach me how to make French pastry. It sickened her to be in the same room with my sister or me and that never stopped hurting. *Never.* Even now that I know why she came home fucked up and stayed that way, the fact that my mother decided to stop loving me tears me up inside."

"I'm sorry you had to go through that," Clay said, "but I don't—"

"I'm not asking you to feel sorry for me." Harley stood up straighter. "I just need you to understand that I know firsthand what it's like to lose a mother. It's not the sort of thing you grow out of. It's the kind of thing that damages you and leaves you believing that you're not good enough. That you'll never be good enough or worthy of being loved for the person you are."

She paused as a warm breeze swept between them, setting the leaves to rustling overhead, the light clatter of the palms seeming to echo her plea for compassion. "Is that what you want for Jasper? To be abandoned by the only parent he's ever known? And to blame himself for it? Because he will, Clay, it's what abandoned kids do."

He was quiet for a long moment, his eyes searching her face. For what, she wasn't sure, but she lifted her chin and let him look. She had nothing to hide. She was speaking the truth and if he could step away from his anger long enough to think clearly, he would see that she was right.

"What's he like?" he finally asked, the question breaking her heart a little.

It was sad that Clay didn't know his son. It was even sadder that the wonderful man she'd once known had become someone she would be reluctant to leave alone in a room with Jasper.

"He looks like you," she said. "But he keeps his feelings close to his chest like me. He's incredibly smart and curious, but he hates to make mistakes. He likes to do things right the first time. When he doesn't, he gets angry, but in a quiet, private sort of way. He doesn't lash out or get aggressive like some boys. He's...very sweet."

A smile trembled across her face. "He always has been. Since the day he was born. And I've done everything I could to help him stay that way. To help him grow and learn and be happy."

She sniffed, fighting tears as she pushed her hair away from her face, suddenly so exhausted it felt like the light breeze drifting in from the ocean might blow her over.

She was so tired, so very fucking tired. She'd been worn down, worn out, and desperate for a break in the non-stop drama and danger before she ended up here. All she wanted was peace for her and Jasper and if the only way to have that was to cut a deal, then maybe she and Clay could work something out.

But not his deal—hers.

Jasper truly was an extraordinarily sweet, clever kid. He wouldn't do anything to provoke Clay, and Clay seemed to want to keep Jasper safe—surely that extended to protecting his son from his ugly new temper.

"Listen, I know you hate me, and you have every right to." She clasped her hands together in front of her, not too proud to beg if that's what it took to find her way back to her son. "But I never meant to keep Jasper from you. I didn't even know you were alive. Now that I do, we can work together to give him the best life possible. I'm willing to cooperate, even share custody if we can come to an agreement that works for both of us, but I can't desert him. I won't. I know he needs safety and stability, but he also needs his mother."

Clay shook his head slowly back and forth. "You are…a piece of work." He sounded nearly as tired as she felt.

Her shoulders sagged. "Not a good piece of work, I'm assuming."

"You would have been an amazing spy," he said, not bothering to answer her question. He didn't have to. It was clear from the flat look in his eyes that he didn't believe she had anything to offer Jasper.

"I don't want to be a spy," she said bitterly.

"All I want to do is get out from under my father's thumb and Marlowe's thumb and find a safe place for Jasper and me to build a life. I'm trying to work with you, Clay, even though you're clearly out of your damned mind. Why won't you at least try to—"

"You're the one who's crazy if you think happily ever after is in the cards for you." He lifted the Taser, pointing it at her chest. "I told you the day we arrived, you're not calling the shots. You have no power here and you will never convince me that you are anything but walking, talking poison."

Harley fought the urge to lunge for him and pound her fists on his stupid, stubborn chest. Touching him was dangerous—awareness still simmered in the air between them, underscoring the anger like a relentless drumbeat—and she didn't want to get sucked into another encounter unless she had a plan to use his attraction for her to her own advantage. Besides, she wouldn't be able to do much damage with her fists before he Tasered her again, and she couldn't afford to lose any ground she might have gained in the past ten minutes.

Clay hadn't changed his mind, but at least he'd listened to what she had to say and refrained from trying to kill her.

*At this rate, by the time Jasper graduates from high school, he'll be down to slapping you around once a week.*

The thought sent a sour taste flooding through her mouth.

"These are your options," Clay continued in a tight voice. "One, you tell me where Jasper is right now, this very second, and I let you go free. Two, you keep fighting me, giving Marlowe time to find Jasper, and when I get the information I need from you—and I will get it, make no mistake about that—you will go directly into CIA custody. And by then, our son might be dead."

Harley's heart stuttered and her blood went cold, but she refused to let Clay scare her.

Jasper was with Dom, and Dom, for all his goodness, didn't fuck around. He had plenty of experience dealing with bad men and dangerous situations. He would do whatever it took to keep Jasper safe. He would keep his guard up and Jasper out of harm's way and even if she were out of the picture for a while, he wouldn't be in any hurry to drop Jasper off with Jackson and Hannah.

Thank. God.

Jackson was Clay's friend and wouldn't hesitate to hand Jasper over to his biological father. No, sending Jasper to Hannah wouldn't work. Not anymore.

Which meant that Harley had to survive, get out of here, and get to Dom. And then she could plan what to do next, even if that meant spending the rest of her life running from Marlowe and Clay and anyone else who tried to take her son away from her.

Life on the run was its own kind of hell, but she would rather go through hell with Jasper than escape to heaven without him.

Drawing on the last of her strength, she lifted herself up as tall as she could stand in the heavy combat boots Clay had found for her and met his hard gaze. "There are never only two choices. Fate is too fickle to make life that easy for you or anyone else. There are always other options. Always."

"If you're hoping I'll shit myself to death, you'll be waiting for a long time," he said. "I haven't been sick a day since I was discharged from the hospital after the accident."

"I'm rarely sick, either," she said calmly. "I'm too stubborn."

"I know you are," he said, his expression softening the tiniest bit. "But I'm not playing games, Harley. This is your one and only chance to have this end well for you. I won't offer a deal again and every second you spend fighting me is a second that Marlowe gets closer to our son."

"I'm not playing games, either." She stared up at him unflinching, willing him to see that he'd met an immovable force and put them both out of their misery. "I won't let you scare me into abandoning Jasper, and if something happens to him, it will be on your head as much as mine. Compromise is the only way forward. If you can't bend, we're both going to break and take an innocent little boy down with us."

His eyes roamed her face, but he didn't speak, and in the silence, the drumbeat of attraction pulsed louder. She didn't know how it was possible, but she still wanted to pull his mouth down to hers and taste him, even now, when he had proven that he was a stubborn madman intent on putting Jasper's life in jeopardy.

It would make her hate herself if she wasn't already there.

She'd hated herself for longer than she could remember. She'd hated herself as a child for not being able to win her mother's love, she'd hated herself as a young woman for her sick compulsion to destroy every man who came into her life, and she hated herself now for creating this living hell that she was trapped inside. The legacy of her sins was inescapable, and if it were only her life to consider, she might have given up on it a long time ago.

She'd given up on romantic love and a relationship with her sister and love from her parents and recognition for her art and everything else she'd secretly, or not-so-secretly, craved when she was younger. Giving up on breathing wouldn't have been far behind, except for one little boy and the promises she had made to him, promises she refused to break, no matter what fresh hell came seething into her life.

"All right," Clay whispered. "Then break it is."

Without another word, he turned and led the way into a darker part of the jungle.

# CHAPTER SEVEN

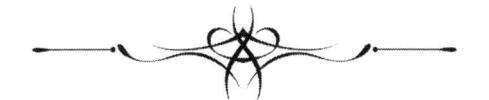

Clay

They traversed the five-mile trail leading to the other side of the island in silence. Clay had no idea what Harley was thinking, but his thoughts were a steady mantra of *don't fuck this up*.

This was the moment when their course would be set, one way or another.

Clay had been involved in enough

interrogations to recognize a turning point when he was in the middle of one. By the end of today, he would have either broken Harley's resolve or she would have double-downed on her silence and committed to seeing it through to the end.

Maybe even the bitter end.

He didn't plan on using enhanced interrogation techniques beyond what was available with the sensory stimulation cell—that kind of torture didn't work; no matter what a few idiots in the FBI seemed to think—but even if he did, at this point he wouldn't put it past Harley to do exactly what she'd sworn to do. She might let herself be water-boarded to death before she gave up Jasper's location.

She was so fucking stubborn.

*That's why you have to make today count. Push slow and steady. She's exhausted and vulnerable and worried about Jasper.*

*This is your shot; don't fuck it up.*

*Don't. Fuck it. Up.*

"Turn right," he said when they reached the third fork in the trail. "We'll take this loop up around the cliffs by the sea and then back around the other side of the island."

Harley obediently turned right, but her boots dragged in the dust as they started up the incline toward the cliffs. He'd found several pairs of tennis shoes in an old storage room, along with scrubs in various sizes and female uniform pieces he could have given Harley to wear, but he'd chosen the boots instead. They were heavy and would wear her out faster, and his boxers and tee shirt clinging to her sweat-soaked skin would help remind her that she was powerless. She was under his control, dependent on him for everything from the food she ate to the clothes covering her nakedness.

But she wouldn't be enjoying the privilege of even humble clothing for much longer.

A part of him hated that it was going to come to this—the fact that he was even considering what he had planned for when they reached the falls on the other side of the cliffs proved he was off the rails. But the other part of him was simply grateful for an excuse to be skin to skin with her again, to take things slow this time and memorize the way it felt to fuck this woman who affected him like no other.

Love her or hate her, Harley got to him. Got under his skin and in his head and drove him fucking out of his mind with wanting her.

He'd been semi-hard all day, just the smell of her drifting to him as he walked behind her on the trail enough to make him ache. It had been hard enough to resist her when she'd been an image on a monitor. With the flesh and blood woman close enough to touch, the temptation to get her naked and underneath him was overwhelming.

Visions of the way she'd looked with her hand working between her legs and her nipples pebbled tight beneath her fingers haunted him, along with fantasies of the way she would arch beneath him as he pushed inside her heat. But this time, imaginary Harley wasn't crying or fighting or cussing him. She was as eager and turned on as he was and just as relieved for a break in the tension vibrating between them.

The shift in the direction of his fantasy

world was a positive sign for his psyche but bad news for the success of this mission. Harley wasn't the only one weakening. For a split second this morning, he had been tempted to see her side of the situation with Jasper.

The flash of doubt had only lasted a moment before he'd reminded himself that it didn't matter if she loved Jasper or if she was right about what losing his mother would do to their son. She was a monster who had lived stupidly and dangerously and put her child in unforgivable danger. Now it was time for her to pay the price for her mistakes.

She should have been behind bars years ago. He wasn't doing anything to her that the American justice system wouldn't do as soon as she was taken into custody. She was going to lose Jasper no matter what.

At least he was going to give her freedom, and a chance to build a life for herself as long as she stayed away from Jasper. There was nothing else he could offer her. More importantly, there was nothing else he should *want* to offer her. He couldn't allow himself to feel pity for a monster. If he did, the monster would only use his empathy against him and Jasper would end up paying the price.

"Can I have a drink of water?" Harley asked, her voice rough.

He'd caught her eyeing the canteen slung across his shoulders several miles back, but she hadn't said a word and he hadn't made any offers. He wasn't here to anticipate her needs or provide for her comfort, something he would do good to remember when they reached the falls.

"In a few minutes," he said. "There's something I want you to see about half a mile up when the trail curves back into the jungle. We'll stop there."

She sighed, but didn't protest and after a few moments her feet began to move faster, making a grim smile stretch across his face. She wouldn't be so eager to reach their destination if she knew what awaited her there. But he was all for speed. He was past ready to have her bared to him, her nipples pebbling beneath his fingers, her head falling back as arousal flooded through her veins.

*And what if she says no?*

Clay dismissed the thought. She wasn't going to say no; she wanted him as much as he wanted her. It was in her eyes every time she looked at him—hate and hunger in equal measure, proving he wasn't the only one infected with this sickness.

Ten minutes later, Harley turned a sharp corner on the trail and froze, her breath rushing out. "Oh my God."

"Pretty, isn't it," he said, coming to stand behind her, gazing up at the narrow falls trailing down the side of the grassy rocks to the wide, peaceful pool below. "I thought you might like a swim."

She glanced sharply over her shoulder but turned back to face the falls just as quickly. "I would like a swim. My feet are on fire. I don't suppose it's safe to drink that water, is it?"

"Doubtful, but you can have some of mine." He circled around her, uncapping the canteen as he moved. "Open your mouth."

She held his gaze, watchful as she tilted her head back and parted her lips. Clay moved the canteen an inch from her mouth before he tilted it, sending a thin stream of water trickling from the opening. Her tongue slipped out, instinctively helping guide the water down her throat. Some of it dribbled down her chin, but she didn't move to wipe it away. She drank greedily, her throat working as she swallowed. By the time he shifted the canteen, stopping the flow of water, he was hard enough to club a baby seal to death with his cock.

Needless to say, he would have to wait to join Harley in the water.

He didn't want her to realize how much power she held over him or that watching her drink had been one of the sexiest things he'd seen in recent memory.

"Should I swim in my clothes?" She held his gaze, her chest rising and falling and her nipples poking through the thin fabric of her shirt.

"You could," he said, "but that would make for an uncomfortable hike back. Wet clothes tend to chafe."

"Then I guess I should swim naked," she said, bending her knees with a graceful, sensuous movement that had Clay's cock twitching in his pants.

So much for hiding his hard-on. There was no way Harley would miss the bulge behind his zipper, not when she was squatting right in front of him.

"Boots first. I've been dying to take these off." She began to work open the laces, keeping her head tilted back and her eyes trained on his. "But I bet you knew that, didn't you?"

He inclined his head but didn't respond. He was too busy admiring the way her shirt gaped at the neck, granting him peek-a-boo glimpses of her tits. She was the perfect handful, with nipples that tilted up, practically begging to be kissed, sucked, trapped between teeth, and teased.

She nodded knowingly. "I bet you chose the heaviest, most uncomfortable pair of shoes you could find, didn't you?"

His lips curved without his permission. He couldn't help himself. He should be angry that she could still read him so well—not long ago he would have been enraged by that smug grin lilting across her full mouth—but sometime in the past two weeks things had changed.

There was an intimacy in holding another human being prisoner. It was an ugly, unbalanced breed of intimacy, but intimate nonetheless. He felt closer to Harley than he had before, close enough that the memory of his fingers wrapped around her throat made his gut twist every time it drifted through his head. If he had damaged her or, God forbid, killed her, he would never have forgiven himself. Those blue eyes were nothing but trouble, but he didn't want to watch them close forever.

"Are you coming in?" she asked, tossing her boots and socks to the side of the trail and sitting back on her bare feet.

"I will," he said. "But I'll wait for you to get in first and stay between you and the trail. Don't want you to get any ideas."

"Too late," she said with a sultry, feline grin. She brought her hand to his thigh before letting her palm skim slowly up until her fingers molded around his erection, squeezing him gently through his shorts. "This is already giving me ideas."

"Is that right?" He kept his expression impassive, determined not to show her how good it felt to have her hand on him. "Anything you're willing to share with the class?"

"Well," she said, bringing her other hand to the close of his shorts, slipping the button free of its hole, making his heart beat faster. "I *am* already down on my knees. It seems a shame not to take advantage of it."

She drew his zipper down before curling all eight fingers around the top of his boxer briefs and tugging them up and over his cock. His swollen shaft bobbed free, already thickly veined and flushed with need.

He wanted her lips wrapped around his cock more than he could express in words. He wanted to cradle her head in his hands and fuck her mouth until he blew down the back of her throat and watch her swallow him down, moaning the way she always had before, like the taste of him was better than chocolate.

But he wasn't a fool. For better or worse, he remembered everything Harley Mason had ever said to him.

So when she moved her lips closer to his cock, he drove his fingers into her hair and made a fist, taking control, making sure she didn't get close enough to do any damage.

Her eyes rolled up to meet his, an unspoken question in their depths.

"Teeth," he whispered softly. "Because blow jobs should involve a subtle reminder of who is in charge."

Her smile burst across her face—unexpected and…beautiful.

She was so fucking beautiful when she smiled like that. There had been a time when he'd lived to make her smile. He'd spent the hours he was away from her thinking of things that would make her laugh, stories to tell her when they were curled together under the covers, exhausted from making love, but not ready to go to sleep, not wanting to let unconsciousness take hold and tear them apart.

"You remember," she whispered, her smile

fading.

"I remember everything," he said, his throat tight. "Everything you said that made me love you when I thought you were someone else."

She held his gaze for a long moment while his cock bobbed lightly between them, like a dog too stupid to know that the moment had soured and the time to play had passed.

Finally, she said, "I won't bite your dick off, okay? I promise."

"Your promises mean very little to me."

"But I want to taste you," she said, her gaze darkening with a hunger that made his balls ache. "I want to suck you until you explode between my lips. I want it hard and fast until I'm drowning in you."

He took a deep breath, ignoring the voice issuing from the general vicinity of his groin that urged him to trust her, just this little bit, just enough to give him the chance to fuck that beautiful mouth.

But he'd learned to ignore that voice a long time ago. Listening with your dick was pure stupid and he didn't have time for stupid today.

Or any other day.

The realization that he would never know the bliss of a Harley blow job again—she truly was a master of the art—made his chest tighten, but his grief was short-lived. There were still so many options left on the table and it was past time to start exploring them.

"Take off your clothes," he said, loosening his grip on her hair. "And get in the water."

"You've gotten bossy in your old age," she said, but she obediently reached for the bottom of her tee shirt and drew it over her head, revealing her perfect, teacup-sized breasts. "Is that just for me or are you an alpha-hole with all the girls?"

"Now the shorts." He stripped his own shirt off and tossed it to the ground. "Stand up and take them off. Slowly."

She stood, a faint grin curving her lips as she hooked her thumbs beneath the elastic waistband of the simple navy boxers and drew them down, inch by torturous inch, revealing the thatch of brown curls between her legs. When the fabric reached her thighs, she shimmied her legs, sending the boxers sliding to the ground to puddle at her feet.

"What's next, boss man?" she asked. "Since you seem to get off on being in charge."

Without a word, Clay stepped closer, slipping his fingers between her legs and driving into where she was already slick and swollen, drawing a soft, and extremely satisfying, moan from her lips.

"And it seems like you get off on being told what to do," he said, fucking her with his fingers—long, slow, strokes that made her head fall back and her lips part. "Or have you been wet for me since this morning?"

"Who says it's for you?" she asked, her voice breathy. "Maybe I've been thinking about someone else, someone with a friendlier dick than yours."

"My dick is plenty friendly." He brought his free hand to her breast, brushing his thumb across her tight tip. "It's the rest of me you have to worry about."

Harley's eyes slid closed. "You brought protection this time?"

He lowered his face to her neck, inhaling

the sweat and flowers smell of her, a combination that made his cock throb with its own desperate heartbeat as he pressed a kiss to where her pulse raced beneath her skin. "Assuming things go that far, yes. But I won't lose control again."

Her lids slitted open, her eyes glittering in the sun filtering through the trees. "Why does that sound like a threat?"

"Get in the water," he said, his voice husky.

*And I'll show you*, he added silently.

# CHAPTER EIGHT

Harley

*G*reat minds think alike. So do devious ones.

Harley knew exactly what Clay was doing—the same thing she'd been trying to do when she'd knelt at his feet and freed his stupid beautiful cock from his shorts—but that didn't keep her traitorous libido from responding. She eased into the cool water beneath the falls with her skin burning and her body aching for more of what he'd started. More of his hands and his mouth and that clever mind that was every bit as sexy as the rest of him.

But if he thought she could be manipulated by a taste of the way things used to be, he was about to learn just how wrong he was.

He could smolder and seduce and boss her around her all he wanted, but she was never going to tell him where Jasper was. She was going to get close to him, get off, and then use his own tactics against him.

He was weakening. There had been nostalgia in his voice when he'd quoted the joke she'd made the first time she'd gone down on him—in the shower, licking him up and down before dragging her teeth lightly along his shaft. And he'd smiled at her, more than once. Maybe they were false, but even forced smiles had power. She had forced a smile for Jasper's sake more times than she could count and discovered in the process that if she kept a grin plastered on her face for long enough she would eventually start to feel happier. Or at least more relaxed than she'd been before.

She didn't need Clay to love her again or even like her; she just needed him to relax his guard long enough for her to take advantage.

Harley picked her way over the smooth stones beneath the water, scanning the pool for signs of danger. But there were no snakes, no large animals lurking in the ferns along the shore, nothing but the frayed ribbon of the falls whispering down, sending ripples out across the pool. Unexpectedly, the water was cool enough to be chilly—unlike the ocean this time of year—but she barely noticed the cold. Her senses were focused on the sound of Clay easing into the water behind her and the way her nerves sizzled in response.

She glanced over her shoulder, the sight of him taking her breath away.

He was even more stunning than he'd been when they were younger. He'd thickened through the shoulders and the cuts defining each dip and curve of his muscular frame had deepened. If she'd been the sort to wax poetic, she could have written a verse or two about the sharp V running up either side of his hips, the veins on his powerful forearms, the sprinkling of golden hair at the base of his abdomen, and the rakish lilt of his cock.

It still curved lightly to the left as if trying to help him hitch a ride to somewhere better than here.

"There's nowhere better than here," she murmured as he closed the distance between them, a predatory look in his deep blue eyes that made her shiver.

"It doesn't matter if there is or there isn't," he said, remembering his response to their private joke. "Here is where we are. And I'm going to make the most of it."

He stopped in front of her, close enough for her to feel the heat rolling off of him in waves and to realize how desperately she wanted his hands on her, his mouth on her.

"What do you want, Harley?" he asked, his voice husky. "How do you want me to touch you?"

"I don't," she lied, even as his pine and soap smell sent fresh heat rushing between her legs.

"So you don't want this?" He brought his hands to her breasts, cupping her in his warm palms before capturing her nipples between his fingers and rolling her taut flesh. "You don't want me to touch you here?"

She bit her lip and fought to hold still. She didn't want to give him the satisfaction of even that small response, but she couldn't help herself. She needed the pain of her teeth digging in deep to keep her back from arching, her thighs from squirming, and her hands from reaching for him.

"Or maybe you would prefer my mouth?" He knelt in the water. Before she could move away, his tongue was flicking across her nipple, sending a wave of heat surging through her core.

Her breath rushed out, but she sucked it back in, holding it trapped in her lungs, hoping it would help her stay strong as he licked and sucked. Licked and sucked…licked and…

"Fuck me," she said with a groan, her resistance crumbling as she drove her fingers into his hair.

He sucked her nipple deep in response, trapping it against the top of his mouth and doing that thing he did. That wicked thing that had once made her come simply from having her nipples ravaged by his mouth. Soon, her breath came in pants and her knees had turned to jelly and still he suckled her harder, trapping her other nipple between his fingers and pinching her in time to the suction of his mouth.

Her womb tightened and her hips began to rock, instinctively seeking friction though there was nothing but water between her legs.

But she wouldn't need much more. She was so close, so fucking close, so—

She cried out, a sharp sound of shock and dismay that tumbled from her lips as Clay abruptly pulled away from her nipples.

A second later, he took her by the arms, spinning her around. "Time to get wet."

She barely had time to pull in a breath before he had pushed her forward, sending her tumbling into a deeper portion of the pool. As her head slipped beneath the surface, she opened her mouth and screamed, giving her rage and frustration to the water, even as she tried to get her body back under control.

She had to regain control, had to firm up her defenses and get ready for a fight.

If she knew Clay—and she did, that fucking bastard—this was only the beginning of her suffering.

FILTHY WICKED LOVE

# CHAPTER NINE

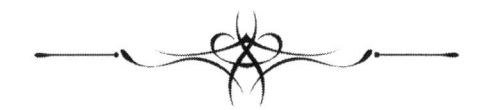

Clay

Harley emerged from the water sputtering, murder clearly written on her features as she found her footing and waded back into the shallow water.

"Or were you already wet?" Clay asked, unable to fight the smile creeping across his face.

"You're an asshole," she said, swiping

roughly at her damp cheeks.

"No, I'm not." She looked fucking stunning with water streaming down her bare curves, a fact that only made him ache to get his mouth back on her that much faster. "I just need you to tell me what you want. Better yet, I want you to beg for it."

She muttered something beneath her breath that sounded like, "Why am I not surprised," but Clay didn't ask her to clarify.

Instead, he crooked his finger. "Come here. We'll try again and see if you've learned your lesson."

"And what if I say no?" she said, intensifying her glare. "Better yet, what if I tell you to go to hell and stick your dick in the first lake of fire you find?"

His lips curved again. "Then you won't get to come, will you? Because the only way you're getting off is on my fingers or my cock or my mouth."

Her eyes flashed, giving her away.

He shifted closer, his bare feet sure on the stones. "Would you like that? My mouth between your legs? Do you want me to fuck you with my tongue until you come so hard I have to hold you up to keep you from sliding under the water?"

She exhaled, slow and ragged. "And if I say yes?"

"That would be a start," he said, reaching up to curl his fingers around the back of her neck. "But I believe I mentioned begging. What is it going to take for you to learn to beg?"

He held her gaze as he took his cock in hand and tilted his leaking tip down to brush against her clit. The sound she made—a cross between a yelp and a moan—was enough to make his cock twitch against her again. Her head fell back, resting against his hand, her breath already coming faster.

"Maybe something like that?" he asked, severing the contact between them.

"Yes," she said softly. "Do that again."

"Do what again?" he asked, wanting to hear it from her lips.

"Rub your cock against me," she said, her eyes hooded. "Tease me. Make me beg you for more."

"Spread your legs," he ordered, still gazing straight into her eyes as he rubbed the head of his dick in slow, firm circles on her clit. If he looked down, he knew the sight of their bodies so close to joining would be hot as hell, but he had to maintain control.

Besides, her eyes were putting on their own show, anger and hunger shifting back and forth like a kaleidoscope spinning in the sun.

"Are you getting wet for me again?" he asked, pushing on before she could respond. "I think I should find out." He dipped lower, sliding his shaft between her lips, fighting a groan as her slick heat coated his skin.

"You want to be inside me so bad," she said, flexing her thighs, increasing the pressure squeezing in around his erection. "You want to bend me over that rock and fuck me hard from behind. You want my hair in your fist and your cock so deep you—"

Her words ended in a bleat of rage as he pushed her back into the deep end of the pool.

What she'd been describing was one of the many fantasies pulsing through his head, but this wasn't about fulfilling his fantasies or letting her take the upper hand. This was about driving her to the edge and making her twist there, about bringing her low and breaking her with her own desire.

This time, she came to the surface swinging. She lunged for him, but he captured her wrists, transferring them both to one hand that he lifted over her head. He held her there, thrashing and cursing his name, as he brought his free hand to her breast, pinching her left nipple hard enough to make her cry out.

It was a sound of pain and pleasure, but it wasn't yet a sound of surrender.

"Fuck you," she hissed, chest rising and falling faster as he plucked and rolled her other nipple. "I hate you so fucking much."

"But you want me even more," he said, his balls beginning to feel bruised with the need for release. "You want me to fuck you against the rocks by the waterfall. You want to feel me moving inside of you, making you take every inch of my cock, making you come so hard you feel like the pleasure is going to rip you apart."

"I'm not, I don't—" She cut off with a whimper, her wrists stopping their squirming to get free. "Please stop. Please stop this."

"Stop touching you?" He trailed his knuckles down her quivering stomach and slipped his fingers back between her legs, teasing through her slick lips. "Stop doing this?" He slid two fingers inside her well of heat, moving in and out as his thumb pulsed on her clit.

"Y-yes," she panted, her eyes squeezing closed. "No!"

"Which is it, yes or no?" He added a third finger and watched her lips part on a sexy little sigh, the kind that had always driven him wild. "Better speak up fast, Harley. I'm not feeling patient today."

"Don't stop," she said, rocking into his hand. "Please don't stop. Please let me come. I want to come."

"You want to come on my hand?" He released control of her wrists, wrapping his arm around her waist and pulling her close enough that he could whisper in her ear as he continued to work his fingers between her legs. "Or do you want my cock, Harley? Do you want me to fuck you again, to be buried so deep you can't feel anything but how much I want you?"

"Yes," she said, adding quickly, "Please. Yes, please. Please fuck me. I want you inside of me."

She reached down, gripping his cock and stroking him up and down, sending heat surging across his skin and desire pulsing through his veins. But instead of hitching her up around his hips and impaling her on his throbbing shaft, he pulled her hand away and brought his hands to her shoulders, putting her at arm's length.

"Then you need to beg," he said, his voice hard. "You need to beg me until I believe that there is nothing you want more than my dick."

Hatred flickered across her features, but the hunger was still there, burning bright, making Clay smile as he brought one hand to his cock and began to stroke himself up and down. "Or maybe you'd rather I take care of this myself? Spare you the trouble?"

Eyes narrowed, she slipped her fingers between her legs, but he had her wrist in his hand a second later. "Bad girl. You know the rules. It's me or nothing, sweetheart." He released her wrist and slipped his fingers back between her legs, curling them this time, beckoning with a come hither motion inside her slick pussy that made her tremble.

Her lips parted and her hands groped for his shoulders, using them to hold herself upright as he massaged her G-spot. He waited until her legs began to shake and the muscles in her arms stiffened, until her hips rocked desperately against his hand and his fingers were drenched with her heat. He waited until soft hungry sounds issued from the back of her throat and her breasts flushed pink as that relief she was so desperate for swung within reach, and then he pulled away, leaving her to sob as she staggered a step forward, nearly losing her balance again.

"Let me know when you're ready to play by the rules," he said, turning his back on her, doing his best not to show how desperate he was to get to one of the rocks at the side of the pool.

He needed to jerk off before he lost control and he was going to have to fucking sit down to do it. His knees were already weak because that's what Harley did to him. She made him weak, made him scattered.

Made him forget that you should never turn your back on a wounded animal, especially one you've personally pushed to the edge.

The hairs on the back of his neck prickled, warning danger, but it was over before he could turn around. One moment he was focused on putting some distance between him and Harley and jerking himself back into his right mind. The next the world went black.

FILTHY WICKED LOVE

## CHAPTER TEN

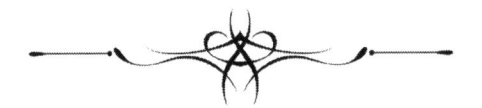

Harley

*E*verything happened in slow motion.

Harley watched her fingers curling around the heavy rock in half time, lived the moment it took for her to swing the lichen-covered stone over her head for a hundred frantic beats of her heart, and felt the clench of her gut as she reversed direction—slamming her makeshift weapon down at a slight angle—for so long it felt like her abdominal muscles were going to pinch in two and squeeze the life out of her.

And then the rock hit Clay's head, a gush of blood burst from the pierced skin at the base of his skull, and time jerked back to normal speed.

Harley cried out as he collapsed, splashing into the pool just ahead of her. Water sprayed into her face and the waves caused by his collapse rocked against her thighs, but Clay didn't jump back to his feet, prepared to take his revenge. He remained facedown in the water, his long arms trailing down to brush the smooth pebbles beneath the surface, his torso rocking gently as the pool rediscovered peace, clearly not overly disturbed by a murder being committed near its banks.

"Shit," Harley whispered, the stone splashing back into the water as her hands began to shake. "Shit!"

He was going to drown. He was going to drown and die. He might still die—she hadn't intended to kill him, just knock him out, but clearly she'd hit him harder than she'd intended—but unless she got him out of the water, death was a foregone conclusion.

She probably shouldn't care that the man who'd tortured her for two weeks was about to die, but his taste was still in her mouth and her body still ached desperately for his touch, and she did care.

Damn her, she did. She didn't want to be a killer and she especially didn't want to kill Clay.

She'd already lived with his blood on her hands for years. No matter how demented a bastard he'd become, she didn't want to live that way anymore.

Bending down, she flipped Clay over onto his back, heart jerking when he coughed and water streamed from his nose and mouth. She froze, ready to drop him and run, but after the coughing had stopped, his eyes remained closed, and after a moment, his breath grew slow and even. Pulse still thready from a dizzying mixture of fear and adrenaline, Harley quickly towed him to the edge of the pool. As the water grew shallow, moving him grew harder, but she managed to hook her arms beneath his armpits and drag his heavy body over the stones and onto the grass at the edge of the pool.

She deposited him as gently as she could and stood staring down at his naked, unconscious form for a shock-numbed moment. And then she turned and ran like hell.

She stopped to scoop her tee shirt and Clay's boxers off of the ground, but she didn't bother with the misery-inducing boots or take the time to dress. Now that she'd made sure Clay wasn't going to drown, she couldn't afford to waste a second.

Terror fueling her weary muscles, she sprinted back down the hill, away from the cliffs, her bare feet slapping against the hard-packed dirt. At the base of the incline, where the path split in two, she skidded to a stop, keeping one panicked eye on the trail behind her as she shrugged on her shirt and yanked the boxers up and over her hips. The forest was still empty, but she swore she could feel Clay coming for her, rapidly eliminating her head start.

*You knocked him unconscious. He's not going to be able to recover from that quickly. He'll be slow and unsteady if he's on his feet at all.*

But her thoughts offered no comfort. Clay was out of his mind, stubborn as hell, and in incredible shape. It was a combination that could work miracles—she should know.

After everything she'd been through, most people wouldn't have the strength left to jog five miles. Harley didn't jog; she sprinted, flying through the woods, leaping over rocks and tree limbs and other obstacles in her path. Her breath burned in her lungs and her legs cramped, but she didn't slow her pace or waste another second looking over her shoulder. She ran like the devil was chasing her out of hell, arms pumping at her sides, her thoughts an endless mantra of *hold on, hold on, hold on.*

She was on her way to Jasper. She just had to hold together long enough to get off this island and everything would be okay. She had a plan in place for emergencies like these. She had passports under three different aliases stored in three different post office boxes throughout Europe, along with enough cash to get her to Prague and Jasper.

She would get to him before Marlowe and then she would figure out what came next. She just had to hold on.

Hold on.

Hold on.

She burst from the woods into the clearing near the cottages and veered left, headed toward the ocean. She hadn't seen anything but the officer cottages and the main building, but this was a military installation. There had to be a dock nearby.

A dock, and hopefully, a boat.

*Please let there be a boat and please let it be easy to hotwire and please let there be water and food on board.*

For a split second, she considered turning back toward the brown and white building where she'd been held prisoner, knowing there was water, food, and other supplies stored inside, but then she saw the dock—and the fishing boat rocking gently in one of the five slips—and kept running.

Freedom was so close she could taste it.

She couldn't bear the thought of going back inside that miserable place and surely she wouldn't die of thirst in the time it took her to get to safety. Clay had transported her here in a day or two. The south Thai islands weren't that far apart and the boat no doubt had GPS.

She trotted out onto the dock, the sun-warmed boards hot on her bare feet, and jumped over the boat's railing onto the deck. The small craft was spic and span, and in the cabin, beneath a storage bench, she discovered a flat of bottled water, packages of almonds, tinned meat, a locked shotgun case, and a box of shells.

Hope and gratitude flooded through her, making her hands shake as she twisted the cap off of a water bottle and tipped it up to her lips. She sat down hard on the floor beside the bench, guzzling the water as she pulled the shotgun case out onto the floor beside her. It was a simple lock, the kind likely to pop on its own if you dropped it on the ground enough times. But there were faster ways to get basic mechanisms like this to give.

She looked up, swiping water from her

mouth as she scanned the rest of the tidy cabin. All she would need was a paperclip or a straw or—

A pen!

She stood, hurrying to the control console, snatching a ballpoint pen from its place beside a leather bound notebook she guessed was the captain's log. With any luck, it would list the location and time of departure from the port Clay had left when he'd brought her here. She would look, as soon as she got the gun open and the boat started and the craft headed out into open water.

Dropping back down to the floor, she twisted the pen apart and pulled out the pressure screw, forcing it straight with slick fingers. She was still dripping sweat, her body struggling to cool her down after the long run. Salty drops streamed down her forehead and into her eyes, but she didn't bother wiping them away. She focused on the lock, jiggling the straightened spring back and forth until the box popped open with a soft *snick*.

A moment later, she had the shotgun cocked open and slid a shell into each of the barrels. She had just snapped it closed and turned to see about opening the boat's ignition panel when she heard footsteps on the dock.

Fast, heavy footsteps, making no effort to be silent as they pounded across the wood.

There was only one person it could be. One other person on this godforsaken island.

Clay.

FILTHY WICKED LOVE

# CHAPTER ELEVEN

## Harley

Heart leaping into her throat, Harley spun around, cursing herself for not getting the boat started first. She might have already been pulling away from the dock right now if she'd hotwired the ignition first.

But she hadn't. She had armed herself and she meant to use the weapon to make sure she got the hell off this island.

Clenching her jaw, she brought the gun to her shoulder, preparing for Clay to burst through the cabin door. She didn't have to wait long. Seconds after she steadied her grip on the rifle, the door swung open, revealing a sweat-soaked Clay wearing nothing but his shorts and boots.

His bare torso glistened and water beaded on his face and neck, smearing the blood that streamed from the wound at the back of his head down over his thickly muscled shoulder. His eyes glinted with rage, but he wasn't out of his mind with it. He still had the sense to freeze when he saw the gun, his gaze darting from Harley to the open storage bench beside her and back again.

"That loaded?" he asked, his breath coming fast.

He must have sprinted the entire way here, too, every bit as eager to recapture her as she was to escape.

"It is. And I'm an excellent shot." She stepped her right foot back, firming up her stance, not wanting to get knocked off her feet by the recoil if she were forced to shoot him. "Even if I wasn't, there's no way I could miss with you this close. The only way you're waking up to see another sunrise is if you get off this boat right now and let me go."

"I can't do that," he said, taking a step closer.

Harley took a mirror step back. "I'm serious, Clay! I will shoot you. I don't want to, but if you give me no other choice, I will. I have to get to Jasper. He's all that matters. Now get the fuck off the boat!"

He shook his head as he slowly lifted his arms into the air in a gesture of surrender she wasn't buying for a moment. "You're right. Okay? You're right. Jasper is what matters. We need to make sure he's safe. Then we can work out the rest of the shit between us."

She tried to laugh, but it got stuck on the way up her throat, emerging as a startled-sounding gurgle. "You know I'm not that stupid."

"I know you're not," he said, edging an inch closer. The movement was so slight most people wouldn't have noticed it. But Harley noticed and it was enough to make her cock the hammer and squeeze one eye shut, preparing to shoot a hole through Clay's gut if he took another step.

He froze. "You're not going to shoot me."

"Don't come any closer," she warned softly.

"If you were going to kill me you would have let me drown," he continued, holding her gaze with his big hands still held aloft, framing his seemingly earnest face. "We were all the way across the pool when you hit me over the head. There is no way I fell at the edge of the bank onto my back. You pulled me there, didn't you? And made sure I was breathing before you ran?"

"I don't want to hurt you, but I will." She fought the tears pressing at her eyes as he shifted another inch her way, ignoring her order, bringing the moment when she would have to kill him to get to her son a second closer. "Please! I just want to leave. Don't make me do this!"

"I'm not going to make you do anything. Not anymore," he said in a deep voice that would have been soothing if she didn't know that he was preparing to pounce at any moment. "You *have* changed. You've proven that. Now give me a chance to prove that I'm not out of my mind. And that I can put Jasper's welfare first. There will be plenty of time for us to fight once we know that he's as safe as we can possibly make him."

He eased another micro-step closer. "I had time to think while I was running back here, hoping like hell that I'd get to the boat before you made it off the island. I get it now, okay. I get that I've been fighting a losing game and that I shouldn't have been playing games in the first place. The second I knew that Jasper was in danger, I should have done whatever it took to keep him safe, even if that meant calling a truce between us."

"You're lying," she said, lips pressing together.

"I'm not," he said. "I swear I'm not, Harley. I swear on my life. On Jasper's life."

Harley swallowed against the salt and fire taste rising in her mouth. She tried to clear her head and think rationally, but the moment was too fraught. All she could think about was the gun in her hand and the man who had imprisoned her and tortured her and used her sick desire for him against her—turning her own body into a traitor that couldn't be trusted—standing in front of her, ready to drag her back to hell.

"I can't go back into that cage," she whispered. "I can't. It will kill me."

"No, it wouldn't." His lips tilted up one side. "You're made of tougher stuff than that. You've proven that, too."

"Don't look at me like that." Her eyes narrowed. "Don't try to trick me. You don't admire me, and you don't want to work together. You just want me to put the gun down."

"Yes, I would like for you to put the gun down," he agreed, shoulders shrugging as his hands began to drift back to his sides. "But I don't—"

He lunged the last few feet separating them, wrenching the shotgun from her hands before she could fire. Her finger hadn't been on the trigger, but even if it had, she couldn't have pulled it. She wasn't capable of killing one of the few people she had truly loved, even if she hated the devil he'd become.

She stumbled back until her bottom hit the control console, and stood, heart pounding, bracing herself for whatever Clay would do next.

Would he shoot her, beat her, or simply fist his hand in her hair and force her back to his torture chamber?

Instead, he opened the gun, shook the shells out onto the floor, and stood staring at her over the evidence of what looked like an attempt at a real truce.

FILTHY WICKED LOVE

# CHAPTER TWELVE

### Clay

There was no other way. This was his last shot.

What he'd said to her was true—he did believe that she had changed. The old Harley wouldn't have hesitated to destroy anyone who got in her way. She would have left him to drown at the falls and never looked back.

*Or maybe not. Maybe you were more than a means to an end, even back then.*

*Maybe she did love you, in her way.*

It was a dangerous, pointless thought.

It didn't matter whether their love had been true or false, the enmity between them now was very real and if he couldn't find a way to defuse it, Harley was never going to take him to Jasper. And that's what would need to happen. She was never going to tell him where his son was hidden. The only way he was getting to Jasper was by taking Harley with him and then only if she trusted him enough to agree to work together.

There was only one thing he could think to do, one way to earn the trust he'd proven he didn't deserve.

"I have footage of you in the sensory deprivation cell," he said, his voice soft and careful in the combustible silence. "We can go back to the installation and you can film my confession that I was the one who put you in there—without orders or the knowledge of my superiors."

Her head turned, but her wary eyes

remained focused on his face.

He took a step back, increasing the distance between them before he continued. "Then you can upload the confession and the footage from the cell to the cloud so you'll have it in case you need to use it against me."

"I won't be able to use it against you if I'm dead," she said, pushing on before he could respond. "But if you'd wanted me dead you could have shot me just now. You need me alive, at least until I take you to Jasper." Her lips trembled but fell short of a smile. "I imagine then all bets will be off."

"That's not true," he said, not surprised that she had worked through the logic of that possible scenario so quickly. "But I realize you have no reason to trust me. That's why you'll have the confession, evidence to prove that I kidnapped you, treated you terribly, and did it all pretending to be on orders from the US government."

Her eyes narrowed, but she didn't respond. She simply watched him as if waiting for the other shoe to drop.

"You could destroy me with even a fraction

of that evidence," he continued. "If I try to trick you or take Jasper away, you leak the video and I'll be on a most wanted list within twenty-four hours."

"And what about the information you have on me?"

"That's my leverage." He leaned against the doorframe leading into the cabin, trying to look relaxed, knowing desperation never played well during a negotiation. "To be handed over to my superiors if you go back on our deal."

"No." She shook her head, sending her still-damp curls rocking around her face. "Then you can take Jasper, leak my file, and—"

"And then we both go to jail," he cut in. "And believe me, I have no urge to spend so much as a night in prison, let alone a decade or more. I was in a coma for eight months. That's enough life lost. I value my freedom. I'm not going to give you any excuse to leak my confession."

Her tongue slipped out, wetting her pink lips. Her entire face was flushed. No wonder, since she'd probably broken a few speed records on her race back to the black site. The color looked good on her, making the exhausted part of him wish they could pick up where they'd left off at the falls, rewind to before he'd taken things too far and just make love in the water.

Fuck *in the water*, he amended. *Neither one of you is capable of more than fucking, and don't you forget it.*

"And what is this deal going to look like, Clay?" she asked. "Because unless it involves me in Jasper's life for the long term, I'm not making any bargains."

"Shared custody," he said. "But we work it out between us, keep things out of the court system. Considering you've been declared legally dead and I've been deep undercover for years, I figure that would be for the best, don't you?"

She frowned, her brow knitting as she shook her head. "I don't understand. What changed between this morning, when I made this exact same suggestion, and this afternoon?"

"You," he insisted, silently begging her to believe him. "Or my perception of you, anyway."

He stepped away from the door, facing her over the shotgun shells rolling drunkenly back and forth on the ground between them as the boat listed on the waves. "You could have killed me, more than once, but you didn't. The fact that you have value for human life, even the life of a man who tortured you…"

He trailed off with a sigh. "Well, that means something. It means a lot. I know that to make co-parenting a child work we're going to have to find more common ground than that, but at least it's a place to start."

Silence fell between them again, but it was a more peaceful silence, the kind that might be broken by birds singing instead of a scream ripping through the jungle.

"Film the confession and help me get it uploaded to safe virtual storage," she said with a breath deep enough to move her shoulders up and down. "After that's finished, you let me stay online and send the man who's guarding Jasper a message that danger could be on the way. When both of those things are done, we can talk about what the future might look like."

"All right." Clay knelt to catch the shells as they rolled toward him. "Just let me lock up the gun and we can head up to the main building."

She watched him as he tucked the shells back into their box and fit the gun back into its case. "You need a better lock on that. If you're planning to have guns in the house when Jasper is with you, you'll need enhanced safety measures. He knows better than to play with guns, but I don't like to take chances. Since he was born, I've stored every one of my weapons in a double lockbox."

He shut the bench lid and stood with a nod. "Sounds smart."

She nodded for a long moment before her features pinched toward the center of her face. "This feels…strange."

"It does," he agreed, feeling more awkward around her than he had since he'd crept up behind her with a syringe in his hand. "But we'll get used to it. People do this kind of thing all the time."

"You think?" She raised a wry brow. "They go from wanting to kill each other in the morning to sketching out co-parenting rules in the afternoon?"

His lips curved. "Judging by the divorces I've been witness to, the killing part isn't far off, but you're right, the swift turn around isn't the norm. Usually, it takes a few months of screaming at each other in a room with lawyers on either side of the table before compromise starts to happen. But we're not divorcing."

"No, I was your prisoner and now I'm not," she said, an incredulous note in her voice. "That's way more fucked up than most divorces, Clay."

"But there are fewer feelings involved." The words felt like a lie, but they weren't.

Yes, he felt different about Harley than he had the day she'd woken up tied to a bed, but that didn't mean he *had feelings* for her. It just meant that he'd let go of some of the rage that had been seething inside of him, poisoning him as surely as anything Harley had ever done.

She was right, he'd been out of his mind with rage. It was only now that he'd begun to move forward in a more reasonable fashion that he was finally starting to feel like himself again, to feel like he was regaining control and ensuring the best possible future for the son he'd never met.

"I have lots of feelings," Harley said, her eyes darkening. "So many feelings, I'm not sure what to name them all, but I do know this: if you betray me, the next time I have a clear shot at you, I won't hesitate to take it."

He nodded. "Understood. And if you betray me, I'll send you to prison for the rest of your life. I don't care if Jasper ends up being raised by one of the miserable, selfish members of your family. If I'm rotting in jail because you released my confession, I'm going to make sure you rot right along with me."

A smile stretched her pink lips. It wasn't the sunshine through the rain smile that took his breath away, but it still transformed her sweat-streaked face into a thing of beauty.

"There, that's the charmer I've come to know," she said, her voice husky. "For a moment there, you were being way too reasonable and level headed."

"Baby steps," he replied, turning back to the cabin door and holding out an arm. "After you."

Harley's eyes narrowed, but after a moment's hesitation, she moved past him and out onto the deck. She remained wary on their walk up to the installation and throughout the setup of the camera in the control room where he'd monitored her cell, but by the time his confession was in the bag and uploaded to her cloud drive via satellite connection, she began to relax.

She allowed him to remain in the room as she posted a blog entry about catastrophic chocolate shortages on the horizon and even laughed when he questioned the choice of topics.

"What could be more terrible than a chocolate shortage?" She stood up from the desk chair, hands on her lower back as she arched her spine. "If that doesn't convey imminent danger, I don't know what does."

"Sore from the run?" he asked.

She nodded. "I don't usually run five miles in bare feet and those boots weren't much better."

"Let me take you to the storage room," he said, moving toward the door. "You can look through the women's uniform pieces and shoes and pick something out to wear after your shower. Or you can have a bath if you'd rather. There's a tub in the bathroom in the infirmary."

He stopped in the hallway, turning back to see Harley standing where he'd left her, studying him with an inscrutable look.

"And what then?" she asked. "Are you going to make me dinner?"

"Dinner should happen," he said, with a shrug. "We don't have to eat it together, but there's a picnic table outside the kitchen that has a nice view of the ocean. We could eat and then start packing up. If we head out tonight, we should reach Bangkok by morning. I've got connections there that can set you up with a passport and we should be able to book a flight to wherever Jasper is."

"I'm not telling you where we're going until we're boarding the plane," she warned as she crossed to the door. "You give me the money and I buy the tickets alone. Agreed?"

"Agreed," he said. "But you never leave my sight, not even for a second."

Harley blinked up at him. "This still feels so odd. It's like you're a stranger. I can't tell what you're thinking."

"That's not that surprising, is it?" he asked softly. "Neither of us was being ourselves before. We were playing our parts, doing whatever it took to get the upper hand and get what we wanted. It was all lies and dirty games."

"Not all of it," she said, sadness creeping into her tired eyes. "Some of it was real. You know that, even if you won't admit it."

Longing and regret swirled through his chest. Agreeing to a truce had made things more civilized between them, but it had also taken touching her off the table. And damn him, but he still wanted to touch her. Maybe even wanted it more than he had before. He wanted to learn what it would be like to fuck her without all the drama in the way, for it to be just him and her and enough pleasure to mute the pain of the past.

They would never escape the ugly legacy of the choices they'd made, but maybe they could turn down the volume. He already knew how good it would feel to have her soft and willing beneath him, wrapping her long legs around his waist and pulling him deeper, closer. He could almost hear the hungry little sounds she would make as he brought her over, smell the scent of her flooding through his head as he fought the urge to come, wanting to feel her clench around him again before he lost himself.

If he reached for her, he sensed that she would let him do all the things he was dying to do to her, but he couldn't take a single step down that road. That road led to emotion and complications and wanting more from Harley than she could ever give, even if she wanted to.

She was who she was and there was no changing that. He could find things to admire about the person she'd become and admit that she'd proven that even monsters could become something better than they'd been before, but she was still the person who had used him to ruin his best friend's life. She was still a woman who had lied to him, played him, and framed a man for a crime he hadn't committed before running off to start a career as a drug smuggler.

There was no coming back from the things she'd done. Her God, if she had one, might forgive her, but he never could.

And so instead of leaning down to capture her lips and learn if she tasted different without hate simmering between them, he tilted his head toward the stock room down the hall. "Come on, let's find you something else to wear. I'm sure it will feel good to get out of those clothes."

She dropped her gaze to his feet with a soft laugh. "Yeah. That's what I thought."

Clay didn't respond, he simply turned and walked away, knowing it was the best thing he could do for the both of them.

# CHAPTER THIRTEEN

Harley

*Two days later*

They touched down in Prague midmorning and fetched the key to the apartment from a PO box near the airport. By noon, they were getting into their third cab and completing their circuitous route to the apartment where Dom and Jasper were staying.

Harley didn't sense that they were being followed, but it was best to be careful. While they were in Bangkok, Clay had been in touch with his associates at the CIA. They'd confirmed that Marlowe had been in south Thailand a couple of weeks ago, only days after Harley had been kidnapped. Even if Clay hadn't taken her away, Marlowe's early arrival would have surprised her. There was a chance she wouldn't have had time to erase all evidence of Jasper's existence before her boss arrived.

The knowledge made her less angry with Clay than she'd been before, taking her rage level down to…Not Really That Angry At All.

In the past two days, Clay had been a complete gentleman. He'd cooperated, kept his promises, and been unfailingly polite, even when she insisted they spend a few hours shopping for clothing in Bangkok, ensuring she, at least, had something appropriate and nondescript for the journey to Prague. None of the shops had sizes large enough to accommodate Clay's shoulders, but he had other clothing with him aside from a castoff pair of scrubs.

No, Harley had no reason to complain about his behavior, but she couldn't help being frustrated by it. The moment they'd agreed to work together, a wall had come down behind his eyes. She knew she should be grateful that he had seen reason—and she was—but she didn't like being shut out.

It was madness to prefer the insane Clay who'd kidnapped her and fucked her in the dirt to respectful Clay who held the door open for her as she slid out of a taxi.

But she had never been particularly sane or reasonable, especially where this man was concerned.

"They're on the tenth floor," she said, clutching the handle of her small leather suitcase tight as she started around the block.

"I'm assuming there's more than one point of entry?" Clay asked.

Harley nodded. "The penthouse has access to the landing pad on the roof in case of the need for air extraction and there are three exit points—the elevator used by all the residents, the main staircase, and a separate servants' staircase that was blocked off from the rest of the building when it was renovated several years ago. Now that entrance only services the penthouse. That's where we'll go in."

Clay kept close as she slipped into the alleyway between two late nineteenth century buildings, shortening his stride so that he remained just a pace behind her, ready to draw down on any threats approaching from ahead or behind. He carried his bag in his left hand, leaving his right free to reach for the weapon hidden beneath his weathered leather jacket.

After a brief argument during which Harley had made it clear that she knew her way around a gun, Clay had convinced her to seek cover at the first sign of trouble while he took care of any deadly force. He was a CIA agent, after all, with more legal loopholes to slip through to get away with shooting someone on foreign soil. Harley would have a much harder time explaining herself if she were caught with a smoking gun.

"Should you call ahead?" He stopped

beside her, scanning the alley while she slipped the key from her jacket pocket. It was still cool in Prague in June and she was grateful for the light cotton jacket and thick linen pants she'd purchased in Bangkok. "To make sure your man knows I'm not a threat?"

"He'll know you're not a threat." She unlocked the door and stepped over the marble threshold into a tasteful entryway. "And he's not my man. He's his own man. He's watching Jasper as a favor. I don't give him orders, so don't assume he'll take them from you, either."

Clay grunted as she locked the door behind them. "I didn't plan on giving any orders, but that's good to know."

"Just wanted you to understand the lay of the land." She started up the stairwell, which was decidedly more rustic than the tasteful entryway where servants from another age would have received packages and sent out messages to other members of Prague's higher society. "Dom can be touchy, but I can handle him. Just let me do the talking."

She glanced back over her shoulder, not

surprised to see tension in Clay's expression. "And relax. Everything's going to be fine. Jasper will be thrilled to meet you."

"I am a little nervous." Clay let out a long slow breath. "What if he wants to know where I've been the past six years?"

"Then we'll tell him the truth. That I thought you were dead and you thought I was dead." She scrunched her nose. "We'll leave out the part about you kidnapping me and me knocking you unconscious. No need to scare him."

Clay's fingers captured her elbow and tugged lightly, stopping her on the landing. It was the first time he'd touched her since that day in the pool. Harley's pulse spiked in response, but when she turned back to him, she was careful to keep her expression neutral. She refused to let him know that she was still attracted to him, not when it was clear he had shut down that part of himself and locked it away.

It was for the best—this was going to be confusing enough for everyone involved without her and Clay hate-fucking on the side—but she couldn't help regretting that she would never touch him again. Never feel his skin hot beneath her fingertips or learn what it would be like to kiss him without any secrets or lies getting in the way.

"Thank you. Really. I..." His hand fell away from her arm. "I appreciate you making an effort to help this go well."

"Why wouldn't I?" she asked with a shake of her head. "I want Jasper to have a good relationship with his father."

She crossed her arms, the better not to take his hand and give it an encouraging squeeze. "And I'd have to be a pretty outrageous hypocrite to hope to be forgiven for the things I've done without offering forgiveness to other people in return. You know what I mean?"

"You really forgive me?" he asked, a vulnerable note in his voice she had been fairly sure she would never hear again.

She glanced up, a shiver working through her as a current of awareness arced through the air between them. It was thin and delicate—nothing like the lightning strike that had exploded between them on the island—but it was something, a sign that maybe he wasn't as immune to her as he'd seemed for the past two days.

"I'm working on it," she said honestly. "The confession and the past two days have helped a lot, and I have a feeling seeing Jasper will finish the job. I can't wait to give him a hug." She sighed, fighting a wave of emotion. "Let's go. I'm excited for you to meet him, too."

Shadows flickered behind his eyes, but he nodded. "Okay."

At any other time, Harley might have stayed on the landing, pressing him until she learned if it was something other than nerves making him look like his dog was on its way to be put down, but right now she was too eager to get upstairs.

Jasper was so close. In a few minutes, she would have him in her arms again.

She took the stairs two at a time and arrived at the door breathing hard, but she couldn't make herself wait to catch her breath before she knocked. She gave the special rap—three short, swift knocks, two slow, and then three fast again—and bounced on her toes, waiting impatiently for Dom to make it to the door, knowing better than to surprise him by letting herself in.

When he opened the door, she hurled herself into his arms, hugging him hard enough to make him grunt. "Thank you for making me get into shape," she whispered into the warm curve of his neck. "You're the very best."

Dom grunted again, his body stiffening even as he returned her embrace. "And who's this?"

"An old friend," Harley said, releasing Dom and searching the wide, airy apartment behind him for Jasper. "I'll explain after—"

"Mama!" Jasper appeared around the corner leading out of the kitchen. He dropped the toys he held—Sasquatch in one hand and chicken pox teddy in the other—and sprinted across the room, a smile lighting up his face.

She squatted down and held out her arms; he crashed into them with enough force to send them both rolling to the floor.

"Hey, bug," she said, fighting tears as he squirmed into her lap and hugged her tight. She returned the embrace, knowing there was nothing in life more precious than hugs like these. "Oh man, I missed you so, so much. I've been thinking about you all day, every day."

"Me too," he said, arms tightening around her neck. "I was so worried. I thought something bad had happened."

"Why would you think that, baby?" Harley petted his hair as she lifted curious eyes to Dominic's face. But Dom only shook his head slightly and returned to side-eyeing Clay like it was his job.

"I've been having bad dreams." Jasper pulled back to look at her, a furrow between his pale brows. "I hate bad dreams. I hate how they feel so real until the sun comes up."

"Me too," Harley said, kissing his forehead. "But now I'm back and I bet you won't have any more bad dreams."

"And if I do I can come sleep in your bed." Jasper grinned, mischief sparking in his eyes.

Harley laughed as she hugged him close

again. "Yes, you can come sleep in my bed, but only for a night or two. With the way you kick, I'd be black and blue if we had too many sleepovers."

"I don't kick in my sleep," Jasper said indignantly.

"How would you know?" Harley said, ruffling his hair. "You're asleep."

"Watch it, lady," he said, smiling as he rubbed his forehead against her shoulder.

"I'm not a lady, I'm your mother," she murmured, her heartbeat finally starting to return to its normal rhythm.

He was here, he was safe in her arms, and they were both going to be okay. Jasper would adjust to the idea of a father in his life, and she would eventually stop worrying that she was making a huge mistake. This was the only way forward. She either let Clay into Jasper's life in a controlled, cooperative manner or destroyed herself trying to keep him out.

Besides, she could do worse than a CIA agent for an ex. At least she could trust him to take the necessary measures to keep Jasper safe.

"So, I'm sure you noticed that I brought someone to visit," Harley said, patting Jasper's back as she pulled away from their embrace. "Would you like me to introduce you?"

Jasper gazed shyly up at Clay. "Okay."

Harley stood, holding onto Jasper's hand, more nervous than she thought she would be. The fact that Dom was standing there scowling at her like she had brought a rabid dog into the apartment wasn't helping things.

Maybe she should have called ahead to warn him, but she'd known there was no way to explain something like this over the phone. She would pull Dom aside and talk him off the ledge as soon as she could, but first, she had to get the hardest part of this out of the way.

"Clay, this is Jasper," she said, pausing to clear her throat before she pushed on with a smile for Jasper's sake. "Jasper, this is Clay. I was told that he'd passed away a long time ago, but he's alive. He found me on the island after you left and couldn't wait to come see you. He's your father, the one I never thought you would be able to meet."

"Really?" Jasper's eyes went wide as he gazed up at Clay.

"Yes. Really." She fought the urge to wince at how awkward she sounded, refusing to look at Dom, whom she could feel shooting daggers at her from over Clay's shoulder.

Clay knelt down, putting himself at Jasper's level. "Hi, Jasper. I'm so happy to meet you. Your mom has told me so many great things about you."

Jasper's shy smile widened. "She brags about me sometimes."

Clay smiled back, his grin a mirror image of his son's. "Well, that's what moms are supposed to do, right?"

Jasper nodded. "Do you have a mom?"

Harley laughed. "Of course he does, Jasper. Everyone has a mom."

"But his mom would be my grandma," Jasper said, shooting her a "duh, Mom" look.

"Yes, I have a mom," Clay said, the awe in his eyes putting Harley's fears at ease. Clay wasn't going to hurt Jasper. He was going to love him, the way a father should. "And she's going to be so excited to meet you. She'll spoil you rotten and make you her famous rocky road cookies."

"I don't want to be rotten," Jasper said. "But I've always wanted a grandma. Does she have gray hair like grandmas in cartoons?"

"No, she has blond hair like us," Clay said. "And the same blue eyes."

Jasper beamed, apparently liking that response. "Do you want to come see my toys? I have an ugly toy collection and some new puppets and cars that Dom and I got at the toy shop."

"I would love to see your toys." Clay glanced uncertainly at Harley as Jasper took his hand, seeming surprised that this was going so smoothly.

"Yeah, you two go. Have fun," she said, before adding in sotto voce. "Kids are less complicated. Just go with the flow and you'll be fine."

"I'm complicated sometimes," Jasper said, grabbing her hand, making it clear he'd heard every word. "Come on, Mama. You come too. I want to show you my dinosaur puppets."

Harley gave his fingers a squeeze. "I'll

come in just a second, babe. Let me talk to Dom first and I'll be right in."

"Okay." Jasper dropped her hand and began towing Clay across the room, the novelty of having a father overshadowing the return of the same old mom who had been around forever.

Harley watched them go until they were around the corner and then turned to face yet another very angry looking man.

It seemed angry men were her lot in life lately.

## CHAPTER FOURTEEN

Harley

Five minutes later, after the pithiest of updates, Dom was even angrier.

"So he kidnapped you, tortured you, and threatened to send you to prison for the rest of your life, and you decided it would be a good idea to bring him home to meet the kid." Dom shook his head as he shouldered past her, heading toward Jasper's room. "Are you out of your fucking mind?"

Harley grabbed his arm and dug her heels in. "I didn't have a choice!" she whisper-shouted. "And keep your voice down. I don't want Jasper to hear. There's no point in scaring him. Clay is a fact of our lives now, like it or not."

"Not. Definitely not." Dom shrugged her off but thankfully stayed where he was and lowered his voice. "This is crazy, Harley. You can't trust a man like that. Especially one who's with the CIA. He has the power to make you drop off the face of the earth. You get that right?"

"I do," she said. "But that's why I have his confession stored in a safe place and I'm going to give you and Louisa the log-in details in case something happens to me. If he crosses me, I can cross him right back. I didn't go into this blind, Dom. I know better than to trust someone I barely know."

"You're trusting him with your son." Dom shot a worried look over his shoulder. "What's to keep him from hurting Jasper the way he hurt you?"

"Jasper is an innocent child. *His* child," she said. "I'm the woman who turned him against his best friend and framed Jackson for rape. Clay has every reason to be angry with me, he has no—"

"Angry, yes," Dom interrupted, brows drawing tighter together. "He can be angry all he wants. That doesn't give him the right to kidnap you or hurt you."

He stepped closer, lifting his hand to her face, tracing her cheekbone with a gentle thumb. "You look like hell, H. I knew you'd been through something the second you walked through the door. I thought the Bangkok deal had gone wrong or something, I never—"

"The Bangkok deal never happened." She eased away, her stomach clenching into a hard knot in response to Dom's touch. Leave it to her sick libido to be repulsed by a decent man while craving the psycho in the other room like a breath underwater.

"And I didn't have the chance to clean out the house before Marlowe showed up," she continued, running a hand through her hair and fisting the strands away from her face. "He was on Ko Tao two days after Clay took me away. That's why I posted the warning blog. I'm pretty sure Marlowe knows about Jasper and that's he's looking for both of us."

"Then we find a place to hide," Dom said, a hard look in his eyes. "You, me, and Jasper. We'll go so deep underground only the moles and the worms will have a clue where we are."

"I can't." She bit her bottom lip, knowing Dom wasn't going to like what she had to say next. "I promised Clay that we'd stay together until his leave is over in a month or so."

Dom's eyebrows crept higher on his forehead. "Together? What the fuck does that mean?"

"Just that he can stay with us wherever we go next," she said with a shrug. "So he can get to know Jasper. That's all."

"Okay," Dom said, studying her with those dark eyes that didn't miss a beat. "Because for a moment I thought maybe you were sleeping with him."

She felt her face flush and hated Dom a little for that sharp gaze of his. "Who I sleep with is my own business."

He reared back, her words evidently enough to send him rocking on his heels before he regained his equilibrium. "You have got to be fucking kidding me," he said in a rough, raw voice. "You fucked him? Please tell me you didn't fuck him, Harley. Please tell me you have more self-respect left in you than that."

"We both knew it was over between us when you left the island," Harley said, anger making her cheeks burn even hotter. "I appreciate your help with Jasper, I really do, but your feedback on who I do or don't fuck isn't solicited. Or appreciated."

"I don't give a shit if it's appreciated," he said, shaking his head back and forth as his lip curled. "Someone has to tell you that you're out of your goddamned mind. Just like your sister."

He laughed an ugly laugh that made her regret letting things get more than friendly between them. "I wish I'd known the only way to win a Mason girl's heart was to beat her and lock her in a cage. I could have kept you on a leash and spanked your pretty ass before bed every night. Then you would have stayed with me and been safe from men like this psycho you're so excited to play house with."

"I'm not playing house with him," she snapped, fighting to keep her volume under control. "I'm doing what I have to do to keep my son. It's called compromise, Dom. It's what adults do instead of throwing a fit when they don't get what they want."

Dom's eyes flashed. "Compromise? Sounds more like a deal with the devil to me," he said, his words hitting too close to home. "But that's what you do, isn't it? You bounce from one bad idea to the next, somehow expecting the next monster you trust to be different than the last one."

He stepped closer, leaning down to whisper his next words into her face. "You realize that's the definition of insanity, right? Repeating the same behavior while expecting a different outcome?"

"Maybe you're right," she said, a hard smile curving her lips as the urge to hurt him the way he was hurting her grew too strong to resist. "I mean, you're certainly not the nice guy you pretend to be. But then I always figured your 'love' for Jasper would go out the window the second I stopped fucking you."

His next breath huffed out from deep in his chest. "You're such a bitch."

"You say that like it's news," she said, ignoring the pain and regret swirling through her.

"I love that kid," Dom said, his forehead wrinkling. "And I would do almost anything to keep him safe, but I can't do this. I can't stay here and watch you make this kind of stupid, dangerous decision."

He swallowed, his throat working. "And I won't watch you with another man. No matter how angry I am right now, I still care about you. And I know without a doubt that I'm the better choice." He shook his head, hurt flashing in his eyes. "It should be me, Harley, and you know it."

Harley pressed her lips together, fighting a wave of regret and self-loathing strong enough to bring her to her knees. "I know," she finally said, voice cracking. "But it's not. It's always been him, Dom. I can't help it. If the past two weeks haven't changed that, nothing ever will."

Dom cursed as his chin dropped to his chest. "You tear me apart, H. You really do. You and your sister." He took a step back, his gaze still glued to the floor. "Say goodbye to Jasper for me."

"Dom, no," she said. "Don't leave without saying goodbye to him. I didn't mean to—"

"It's better this way," he said, still backing away. "And don't worry, I'll take care of the other business we talked about. Even if the girl is as hopeless as the rest of her family, she deserves a get out of hell free card."

"Just give me a month or two and I'll be able to help you," she said, though she felt terrible for consigning the little half-sister she'd never met to even another sixty days of captivity. "Dom, please. The CIA is closing in on Marlowe and the rest of the cartel. I could be free to move around like a normal person by the end of the summer."

"You'll never be free," he said, reaching for

the door. "I think you've made that pretty fucking clear."

Harley lifted her hand, but let it fall back to her side without saying a word. She couldn't reach out to him, not when she had nothing to offer him. At least nothing that he wanted.

Instead, she watched Dom walk out the door with nothing but the clothes on his back. He hadn't even taken the time to pack his bags. That's how desperate he was to get away from her. She had pushed another perfectly good person out of her life and now she was alone, without a single friend in the world, or anyone by her side except a man who had nearly killed her less than three weeks ago and a little boy who needed all the friends he could get.

She was about to go after Dom, to beg him to stay for just a few more days for Jasper's sake, when Clay's voice sounded behind her.

"I'm sorry about your friend."

She turned to find him standing near the island in the kitchen, watching her with a shuttered expression. Jasper, thankfully, was nowhere in sight.

"How long have you been there?" she asked, sniffing as she swiped tears from her cheeks. She hadn't even realized that she'd been crying, that's how emotionally sound and capable of making good decisions she was right now.

"Long enough to hear more than I should," he said, his forehead furrowing. "And I'm sorry about that, too."

Inside, Harley cringed, but she tried to smile anyway. "Yeah. Well, it is what it is, right?"

She crossed her arms and stared down at the floor, willing herself to pull it together. She was so focused on squashing the waves of emotion rising up to drown her alive that she didn't realize Clay had crossed the room until his fingers wrapped gently around her upper arms.

She glanced up, seeing the same longing and regret in his eyes that rushed inside of her, making it hard to breathe.

"It's like that for me, too," he said softly. "It was always you, ever since that summer. I know the situation is too fucked up now for that to make a difference, but…you're not alone."

Her eyes filled again. "Then why do I feel like my last friend just walked out the door?"

Clay's lips parted, but before he could speak, Jasper called out from the other side of the room. "Come on, Clay, I'm ready. You come too, Mom. I'm going to do a puppet show. I just needed a few minutes to practice."

Harley leaned around Clay to grin at Jasper, blinking her tears away. "I can't wait. We'll be right in." She kept her grin plastered in place until Jasper disappeared around the corner again. Then it fell away, leaving her and Clay alone with the hopeless, heartbreaking things they'd said still lingering in the air between them.

"I won't hurt him," Clay said. "You don't have to worry about that. Not now, not ever. He's such a sweet kid."

"He is pretty great, isn't he?" Her chest loosened as she thought of Jasper.

She still had her son. As long as that was true, she could get through anything. She had to get through it. Get through it and thrive on the other side. She wasn't going to let Jasper down now, not when they were so close to having their freedom and a shot at a normal life.

"He is," Clay agreed before adding in an almost shy voice, "Do all parents fall in love at first sight?"

She smiled up at him, a real one this time though it still felt sad on her lips. "I don't know, but I did. The moment I saw his face."

*Kind of like the moment I saw yours.* But she knew better than to say that aloud.

Clay was right. Things were too fucked up now for any amount of emotion—past or present—to make a difference. She would simply have to move on, and pretend she was fine until that unreachable place inside of her froze over again.

It would, sooner or later, and then it wouldn't hurt that she and Clay would never be anything but strangers who had missed their shot at forever.

## CHAPTER FIFTEEN

Clay

They ate a late dinner at the kitchen table, overlooking Prague's fairy-tale view of spires reaching toward the blushing sky and the castle on the hill keeping watch over the people below. Harley made orange and rosemary goose served with glazed carrots and fresh bread from the bakery downstairs, and Jasper shocked Clay by eating every bite of the not-so-kid-friendly food and asking for seconds of the carrots.

His son was smart, sweet, funny, and ate his vegetables without threats, meltdowns, or bribes. He was sure Jasper had his faults like everyone else, but so far Clay couldn't see them.

Even his resistance to going to bed on time was charming.

"But I need to stay up to see all the stars come out," Jasper said, yawning as Harley helped him into his pajamas. "I'm learning the constellations. I need to show them to you, Mom. If you're lost at sea, you're going to need this information."

"I'm sure you're right," Harley said. "But the stars will still be there tomorrow."

"Not if there's a storm," Jasper countered though he obediently lifted his arms so Harley could strip off his tee shirt and replace it with a soft-looking pajama top with an octopus holding eight paintbrushes on the front. "You can't see the stars if there are clouds in the way."

"Good thing we're supposed to have

beautiful weather for the next week then, isn't it," she said, patting his bottom before pointing toward the bed. "Up you go. You're obviously beat, buddy. Get good rest tonight and you can stay up late tomorrow and show me the constellations."

Jasper turned and climbed up on the big white bed. "Clay too? He's not going to leave like Dom?"

"Yes, Clay too," Harley said, shooting a quick sideways glance his way before her gaze returned to Jasper. "Lay down and I'll tuck you in tight, just the way you like. No room for wiggles."

Jasper sighed happily. "Good. Dom never got the covers tight enough."

Harley stiffened, but didn't say a word or turn to look at him again. Things had been even more awkward between the two of them since this afternoon, but he was glad he'd overheard her argument with Dom. Knowing that what they'd shared all those years ago had altered her as profoundly as it had altered him didn't change the present, but it firmed up the moorings of the past.

For the first time in years, he felt like he could trust his emotional intuition.

Harley might have told hundreds of lies that summer, but that one thing—the love they'd felt—had been real. He hadn't been a fool conned by a monster. He had just been a man who had fallen in love with the wrong girl, a wild, dangerous, unbalanced girl with a lust for revenge that had shattered both of their lives, but at least the girl had loved him back.

He hadn't been wrong about that. So maybe, somewhere down the line, when all the chaos and upheaval was behind him, his heart could be trusted to start looking for love again.

"I'm going to head to bed, too," Harley whispered as she closed the door to Jasper's room gently behind them. "All the stress and the travel finally caught up with me. Do you want the front room, and I'll take the one here by Jasper?"

Clay nodded. "Sounds good. Good night."

"Good night," she said, hesitating the barest second before she moved past him, her sweet, sad smell swirling in the air, making him wish he could pull her into his arms and just…hold her.

Just for a little while.

Instead, he kept his arms at his sides and watched her disappear into the bedroom down the hall. Wanting to fuck her was bad enough. Wanting to draw her close and lend her his strength was dangerously stupid. Not to mention cruel. It would be cruel to pretend he had anything real to offer her and he no longer had any urge to be cruel to this woman.

But that wouldn't stop him from doing what he had to do.

Jasper had always been his top priority. Now that he'd actually met his son, he refused to allow anything to interfere with his efforts to keep him safe, not even his growing sense of obligation to the mother Jasper clearly loved to distraction.

Love was well and good, but love didn't stop bullets or disarm bombs. Putting love first was a luxury reserved for people who weren't on a drug lord's hit list. Maybe in six months or a year, when Marlowe was behind bars and his thugs rotting there with him, it would be safe to rearrange his priorities, but for now he and Jasper would both be choosing safety over sentiment.

It was the right choice, the only choice.

So why did it feel so completely shitty?

His chest tight and his thoughts locked into a holding pattern that ensured sleep was nowhere in his near future, Clay showered, changed into pajama pants and a tee shirt, and went out onto the balcony to watch the city lights flicker to life beneath him.

At nearly ten o'clock, dusk still lingered on the horizon, a gentle purple-rose blush that kept him at the balcony railing, watching the light fade as the air turned cool enough to lift the hairs on his arms. He wasn't ready to let go of the day just yet. The city was beautiful, danger was distant for now, and his stomach was resting happily after a wonderful meal with a beautiful woman and an amazing little boy he was lucky enough to call his son.

If only there was just this, just the sky and the city below it and a safe place in between where three people could figure out what they were to each other, maybe there could be something more.

Something…good. Better than good.

The balcony door opened behind him. "I'm sorry," Harley said softly. "I didn't know you were out here. The shades are all pulled on the windows."

"It's okay." He turned to see her standing in the doorway wearing the black tee shirt and silver pajama bottoms she'd bought in Bangkok, her hair in damp curls around her shoulders. "Come out. I don't mind."

She closed the door behind her, crossing her arms against the chill as she padded over to join him at the railing. Her eyes scanned the horizon, but he kept his gaze on her—on the lips that looked even softer than usual, the translucent skin around her clever eyes, and the determined chin jutting out from her heart-shaped face daring the world to take its best shot.

She had been beautiful today with her makeup and jade earrings bringing out the green flecks in her eyes, but fresh from the shower she was stunning. There was only her, bare and vulnerable, with nothing to hide behind and nothing to distract from her perfection.

She was lovely. Perfect—at least to him.

He suspected that no other woman would ever be as beautiful in his eyes as she was, not even if he were lucky enough to get another chance at love. Harley had captured his imagination so completely that he would never be free of her.

But maybe that was okay, too.

Maybe some memories aren't intended to be left behind but instead carried with us as a reminder that there are moments when love is like magic, transforming the landscape of our souls forever.

She sighed, a sad sound that echoed through the melancholy places inside of him. "It's so beautiful."

"It is," he murmured, gaze fixed on her face.

He was still memorizing the delicate curves of her profile when she turned to him. Their eyes met and held and all his noble intentions evaporated in the face of the need to touch her, just one more time.

He lifted his hand, cupping her cheek, his thumb tracing the angle of her stubborn chin. "You are so beautiful."

"Clay," she whispered.

His name was a question he didn't know how to answer, so he didn't. He simply put his arms around her and they came together like they had been made to fit, all their sharp edges dulling as their lips met and they kissed as something other than enemies for the first time in six years.

And it was sweet and soul-stealing and even better than he'd remembered.

His tongue stroked into her mouth and she melted against him, her defenses crashing to the ground as she returned the kiss. Her fingernails dug into his neck as he captured her bottom in his hands and drew her up his body, pinning her hips to where he ached while they did their best to consume each other whole.

Tongues danced, breath sped, and his cock pulsed hungrily against her thigh. Her legs came around his hips and his hand fisted in her hair, pulling her closer as his lips trailed down her neck, kissing and biting. Her soft, hungry moans were enough to make him want to take her right there on the balcony, to strip her pants down her legs and impale her on his cock and let all of Prague hear her scream, but this time he wanted more than fast and furious.

This time, he wanted to memorize every inch of her skin, to make one last memory neither of them would ever forget.

He brought his lips back to hers, kissing her until he swore he could feel her heart beating in his chest and her breath in his lungs and her need dancing across his skin. Flashes of light and bursts of color sparkled and crashed in the darkness behind his closed lids, but he waited until the wanting was almost blinding before he ripped his mouth from hers.

"Can I take you to bed?" he asked, needing to hear the words, needing to know that she wanted this as much as he did.

"Yes," she breathed, legs tightening around

his hips. "Now. Please."

A moment later he was at the balcony door, yanking it sharply open with one hand while he held tight to the woman in his arms with the other. Fourteen long steps and they were in his bedroom, ten more and he was laying Harley down on the bed and lengthening himself above her, his blood rushing as her hands smoothed up his bare stomach beneath his shirt.

"Touch me," she whispered against his mouth. "Please, Clay, touch me everywhere. I need you so much."

He groaned as her hips tilted, her pelvis rocking against where he was hard and hungry for her and only her—his best enemy, his wicked friend, the only one who had ever made him feel like half of something whole.

His shirt vanished and hers followed seconds later and then his mouth was hot on her neck, kissing down to her breasts. His tongue curled around her nipple, teasing her before he drew her deep into his mouth.

Damn, she was so sweet. It was like her skin was covered in sifted sugar, but better because there was the spicy sunshine taste of Harley beneath it highlighting the sweetness, making it something more complicated, more intense, more precious and irreplaceable. He pulled her pajama pants down her legs, desperate to discover the sweetness he'd neglected during the twisted games they'd played in the jungle.

With his hands firm on her thighs, he spread her legs and settled between them, finding paradise and letting himself get lost.

Just this one last time.

## CHAPTER SIXTEEN

Harley

Harley's head fell back and her spine bowed off the bed, lightning dancing across her skin. She forgot how to exhale, how to unclench her fists, how to do anything but spread her legs wider and give herself up completely to the magic of Clay's mouth between her legs.

The man had proven that he could bring

the pain, but now he reminded her that he could also deliver breathless pleasure, the kind of solid gold, drenched in sunshine bliss that made a body forget there had ever been a time when it didn't feel this fucking good. Her breath shuddered out as his tongue flicked back and forth across her clit before he drove the thick muscle into where she was so hot and wet, so swollen and desperate with wanting she wasn't sure she would ever be the same.

"You taste like heaven." Clay cupped her bottom in his hands, his fingertips digging into her ass as he leveraged her closer, giving his wicked mouth unimpeded access.

He licked and sucked and fucked her with his tongue, driving deep and hard while his moans vibrated her clit. Her body coiled like a spring—tighter and tighter, sharper and sharper—until ecstasy cut through her like a knife, severing the ties holding her to the earth. She shattered, heels digging into the mattress as she reached between her legs and fisted thick handfuls of Clay's hair, holding him close as she rocked against his amazing mouth, riding out the waves of the kind of orgasm she hadn't thought she would ever experience again.

By the time she sagged back onto the mattress, her bones had turned to liquid. She offered no resistance as Clay rolled her onto her side and lay down behind her. His hand cupped her thigh, pulling her leg up and back until it was leveraged on top of his and her legs were spread wide enough for him to push into her from behind.

She moaned, arching back as his thick cock speared inside her, spreading her inner walls wide, wider, until she was stretched almost to the point of pain. Her nerve endings sparked electric and she knew she could come again if she let herself, simply from this one agonizingly slow thrust that demanded her complete surrender.

"So beautiful," Clay murmured as his hands found her breasts, kneading and plucking at her nipples as he rolled over onto his back, taking her with him.

Soon she was spread on top of him, one of his hands still tormenting her nipples while the other dipped between her legs to tease her clit and his cock worked in and out, driving her swiftly out of her mind.

"I love this view," he said, his breath hot on her neck. "I love looking down and seeing nothing but you. But us." He pinched her nipple, summoning a gasp from her throat and more heat rushing from the swollen place between her legs.

Clay thrust in hard and deep and she rolled her hips in response, again and again, rocking the head of his cock against the ignition switch deep inside of her. Her breath hitched, but she fought the urge to catch fire, conscious of the fact that he was bare inside of her.

"Condom," she breathed though a part of her couldn't care less about the damned condom.

A part of her wanted him bare, spilling himself inside her, taking a chance on making another Jasper. Another child with his eyes and her stubborn curiosity and pieces of both of them living in harmony, proving they could make beautiful things together.

"It's okay," he said, staying buried deep. "I'll pull out if I get close. I won't lose control tonight, I promise. And I'm not going to go until you come on my cock at least twice."

His hand flattened on her abdomen, pinning her in place as he rocked deeper, each thrust bringing her clit into contact with his fingers, building the tension swelling inside of her to the breaking point.

"God, Clay," she gasped, writhing on top of him as she got closer, closer, and his cock seemed to swell even thicker inside of her. "It's so fucking good."

"The best," he said, squeezing her thigh hard, the hint of pain making the pleasure crest within her. "There's no one like you. I could fuck you forever and never get enough."

His words sent her over. Her back arched as she came, her second orgasm swimming through her veins like electric honey, but Clay wrapped his arms around her and held tight, stroking slow and deep until he'd guided her back to earth and halfway up the next mountain.

"Please," she said, fingernails digging into his lightly furred thighs. "I want to see you, taste you."

With a groan, Clay pulled out and slid from beneath her. A moment later, he was on top, his muscled torso filling her vision as he reached down, gripping his engorged cock and guiding it back to her entrance.

This time, he glided inside without a hint of resistance. She was so wet, so eager, so ready for every long, thick inch of him.

"You're the only thing I could never quit," he said, kissing her with the words as he began to move again, those same luxuriously slow thrusts that made her already pleasure-sated body hum for more. "I tried to end it the second time we went walking on the beach when I realized there was no way I could be friends with someone I wanted the way I wanted you. But I couldn't make myself do it. Not even to do what was right by my best friend."

She threaded her fingers through his hair, holding his gaze as he slid a hand beneath her hips, lifting her off the bed, forcing his cock even deeper into her body. So deep there was nothing but him, nothing but the way they moved together and the things he made her feel and the wild hunger only he had ever sparked to life inside of her.

"I wish it had only been you," she said, wrapping her legs around his hips as his thrusts came faster. "I wish I'd been smart enough to know that this was the only thing worth fighting for."

A pained expression flashed across his features, but before she could say another word, his mouth crashed into hers.

He staked a claim, his tongue gliding deep, imprinting his taste on her soul as he took her hard and fast. He slammed to the end of her, the head of his cock ramming against her cervix, sending a sharp jolt of pleasure-pain coursing through her with every thrust, summoning grunts and groans and other sounds she'd never heard from her lips.

She was wild, unashamed, and so wet she could feel her own sticky heat dripping down her thighs, but she didn't care. She didn't care that she was a hot, shameless, mess. This was the way sex was meant to be, rough and raw and sharp to the touch and so hot the sheets felt like they might catch fire.

"I want to come inside you," Clay growled against her lips as his rhythm grew feverish, wild. "I want to come so hard inside you."

She whimpered, knowing she should tell him no.

But fuck, she wanted it, too. Wanted it even more when his fingers found her nipple and rolled it in tight circles, bringing her perilously close to the edge for a third time.

"I want to push in so hard and deep and feel you milk me dry," he said, slamming home again and again. "God, come for me, Harley. Come on my cock. I need to feel you go one more time."

She cried out as her walls began to convulse around him, clutching so tight it felt like her soul was turning inside out. He answered her with a masculine roar that made her pussy clutch even tighter as he rammed home one last time before he pulled out to come in thick, hot jets onto her stomach.

He gripped his cock, breath hissing out

through his teeth as he worked his jerking shaft up and down, sending more creamy white spilling out onto her skin. The sight was insanely hot—and pulling out had been the sane thing to do—but Harley couldn't help the flash of disappointment that prickled through her.

The animal in her didn't want Clay's release on her belly, it wanted it inside her, filling her up, marking her, making her his.

*His.*

As he leaned down, pressing a kiss to her lips, before whispering—"I'll be right back with something to clean up"—she felt like his. And when he returned with a damp cloth to gently wipe the stickiness from her belly and from between her legs, she felt closer to him than she had to anyone in so long.

She reached out, capturing his wrist before he could head back into the bathroom. "Stay."

His lips twitched, but a smile didn't form. "I was just going to put this in the dirty clothes basket."

"Throw it on the floor," she said, tightening her grip on his arm. "And come back to bed."

"All right." He let the rag fall onto the carpet and climbed onto the bed beside her, propping up on the pillows and pulling her into his arms.

She rested her hands on his chest and propped her chin on top, looking up at his face. It was getting darker in the bedroom, but there was still enough light to see the soft set of his mouth and the easiness in his eyes. "This is the most relaxed I've ever seen you."

His lips twitched again. "Sex is the best medicine."

"Sex with you," she said, knowing now wasn't the time to play games. Now was the time for truth and taking one last, crazy shot at happiness, even if it was a long one. "It's never been like this for me with anyone else. Even years after I thought you'd died, when the worst of the grieving was over, that part of me never came back to life. Never. Until now."

"It's so fucking good," Clay said softly, his gaze fixed on the ceiling. "But it's also bad, Harley. Sex and violence never existed on the same plane in my head until we were together on the island. That first day, when I let my anger get the better of me…"

He shifted haunted eyes to hers. "I scared myself. I've never wanted to hurt a woman and fuck her at the same time. And then suddenly, I did, and it scared the shit out of me. Worse, it made me wonder what kind of man I really am."

She let her fingers play back and forth through the crisp blond hairs on his chest. "They always say there's a thin line between love and hate."

"There's also a thin line between a cop and a criminal," he said, his brows drawing together. "I already crossed that line once. I can't afford a second slip, and I don't want to revisit those fucked up places in my head. I don't want to be that person ever again, not even for another minute."

"You don't have to be." She brushed the hair from his forehead, needing to touch him, to find a way to bring him back to the here and now. "We can put everything that happened on the island behind us and start fresh. We can be good together again."

"Were we ever good together?" Clay pulled away, sitting up and swinging his legs over the side of the bed. "Six years ago we were living a lie—or at least you were—and now we're both different people. You're in deep with a drug lord, and I'm never going to be able to look at your throat and not think about that moment when I had my hand around it, squeezing the life out of you because I'd lost my mind to the hate you made me feel."

"You had every reason to hate me." Harley wrapped her arms around him from behind, her bare breasts flattening against his back. "I forgive you for that. I forgive you for everything. All you have to do is forgive me and we can make this work. I know we can."

Clay sighed, but she pushed on before he could speak, "Because you're right, we are different people. We're people who have hurt and lost and grieved enough to know better than to give up on something real. And this is real." She moved her hand to cover his heart, taking comfort in its steady beating. "Can't you feel it?"

His hand covered hers, warm against her cool skin, pressing her fingers closer to his chest. "I do. But all the rest of the shit is real, too—Marlowe and the past and everything we put each other through. We can't exist in a vacuum, Harley. That's not the way the world works, no matter how much we might want it to."

"But maybe it's the way love works," she said, tears rising in her eyes.

A small voice inside of her demanded to know where the hell her pride had gone, but she didn't care about pride. Pride didn't make her feel alive or hopeful or cared for; Clay did.

"I love you," she whispered, her tears spilling out to dampen his skin. "Even when I started hating you, I still loved you."

He cursed, but when he turned to her, there were tears in his eyes, too.

He didn't say a word to give her hope, but he gave her something better to do than plead for second chances that might never come. He gave her his kiss and his hands bringing her body to life. He made love to her again, sweet and wicked and close, and by the time they were finished, she was too exhausted to do anything but curl against him and fall asleep.

She had planned to sleep with Jasper tonight—to make sure he was safe and close in case Clay got any ideas about breaking his promises—but she wasn't feeling suspicious anymore. She was sated and sad and desperate for a reason to believe that this didn't have to be the last time she ever felt Clay's skin warm against hers.

She slept hard and dreamt of a world where happy endings weren't just for dreamers and people lucky enough not to have been dealt a shitty hand in life. And then she woke up alone in Clay's big bed in the too-quiet apartment with a dry mouth and a pounding head and immediately knew that something was wrong.

Every hair on her body stood on end and a primitive voice deep inside of her shouted to get her ass out of bed.

Now. Quick. Before precious things were lost.

But even before she threw on her pajamas

and stumbled into Jasper's room, fighting the sluggish feeling lingering in her limbs, she knew that he was gone. He was gone, along with his suitcase, his keeper toy collection, and his father, who had vanished without a trace except for a note on the kitchen island with two words written in hasty script—

*I'm sorry.*

With a wounded cry, Harley staggered to her bedroom, terror making her break into a sweat despite the chill lingering in the apartment. She changed into the first clothes she grabbed from the top of her suitcase, snatched her purse from the hook on the door with shaking hands, and less than a minute later, she was out of the apartment and sprinting down the stairs.

She was going to find them. She wasn't going to be too late.

She was going to find Clay before he made it out of the country with her son and then she would make the bastard sorry he had ever been born. She would make him sorry and then she would take Jasper and they would run far away from all the liars in the world.

And once they were safe and sound, she would leak Clay's confession and pray to God he went to jail for the rest of his miserable life.

Harley burst into the alley, the servant door creaking loudly behind her, and raced across the cobblestones. She was so focused on reaching a main thoroughfare and getting a taxi to the airport that she didn't notice the tall man in the black jacket until she was halfway down the block.

Thankfully, the man was on the phone and the dull roar of early morning traffic covered the sound of her footsteps. He didn't seem to hear her racing up the alleyway and when she recognized his profile, she had enough time to duck behind one of the false pillars on the building's edifice before he turned, nodding to a man in a brown flat cap emerging from the bakery behind him.

Harley flattened herself against the cold stones, blood turning to ice in her veins.

She knew the man in the cap. It had been nearly two years since she'd been in the same room with Marlowe—or Liam, his right-hand man—but his wasn't the kind of face you forgot. It was the kind of face that turned dreams into nightmares and assured you all of your carefully thought-out plans were about to turn to shit in your hands.

Marlowe had found her. He must know that she and Jasper were hiding in this apartment building and it was only dumb luck that she hadn't woken up to him standing over her bed with a gun in his hand.

Harley squeezed her fingers into fists at her sides, thoughts racing as she tried to figure out what to do next. She was about to make a break for the other end of the alley—to see if she could slip by whomever Marlowe had stationed there without being caught—when the soft *whup-whup-whup* sound thrumming below the traffic din became a louder *whomp-whomp-whomp*.

She looked up, catching sight of a small black helicopter hovering above the skyline, slowing as it neared their corner of the city and realized several things at once—

1. Clay and Jasper weren't on their way to the airport; they were up on the roof,

waiting for that helicopter to come carry them away.

2. Marlowe might not know his prey was on the run now, but it wouldn't take him long to figure it out—the penthouse was the only apartment with access to the roof or the landing pad.

3. She had maybe two minutes to get up to the roof and warn Clay and Jasper before all hell broke loose.

Not wasting another second, Harley darted out of her hiding place, hugging the shadows as she moved swiftly and quietly back the way she'd come.

She slipped into the servant's entrance unseen, locked the door behind her, and started up the stairs at a sprint, praying harder than she'd prayed in years that she would make it to the roof in time.

Harley and Clay's story concludes in
Crazy Beautiful Love,
Available now.

## Sneak Peek of Book Two
## Crazy Beautiful Love

Warning: This book is a hot and heavy, non-stop, panty-soaking thrill ride that will leave you breathless.

No one betrays Harley Mason and lives to tell about it. For the first time in years, Harley craves revenge—the darker and dirtier, the better—but she has no choice but to put aside her pain and work with the man who deceived her. A precious life depends on it.

His wicked friend, his sweetest enemy—Clay realizes too late that he doesn't want to live without Harley. As they race against the clock to thwart a drug lord, he vows to do whatever it takes to prove his love, even if it means making the ultimate sacrifice.

She needs his help.

He needs her heart.
And neither of them is giving up until they find their crazy beautiful forever.

# Acknowledgements

First and foremost, thank you to my readers. Every email and post on my Facebook page has meant so much. I can't express how deeply grateful I am for the chance to entertain you.

More big thanks to my Street Team, who I am convinced are the sweetest, funniest, kindest group of people around. You inspire me and keep me going and I'm not sure I'd be one-third as productive without you. Big tackle hugs to all.

More thanks to Kara H. for organizational excellence and helping me get the word out. (No one would have heard of the books without you!) Thanks to the Facebook groups who have welcomed me in, to the bloggers who have taken a chance on a newbie, and to everyone who has taken time out of their day to write and post a review.

And of course, many thanks to my husband, who not only loves me well but also supports me in everything I do. I don't know how I got so lucky, man, but I am hanging on tight to you.

# Tell Lili your favorite part!

I love reading your thoughts about the books and your review matters. Reviews help readers find new-to-them authors to enjoy. So if you could take a moment to leave a review letting me know your favorite part of the story—nothing fancy required, even a sentence or two would be wonderful—I would be deeply grateful.

# About the Author

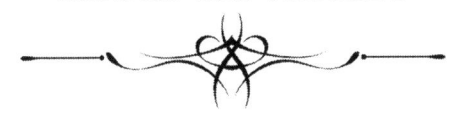

Lili Valente has slept under the stars in Greece, eaten dinner at midnight with French men who couldn't be trusted to keep their mouths on their food, and walked alone through Munich's red light district after dark and lived to tell the tale.

These days you can find her writing in a tent beside the sea, drinking coconut water and thinking delightfully dirty thoughts.

Lili loves to hear from her readers. You can reach her via email at lili.valente.romance@gmail.com or like her page on Facebook https://www.facebook.com/AuthorLiliValente?ref=hl

You can also visit her website: http://www.lilivalente.com/

# Also By Lili Valente

**Sexy Flirty Dirty Series:**

Magnificent Bastard (A Sexy Standalone Romantic Comedy)

Spectacular Rascal (A Sexy Standalone Romantic Comedy)

**The Under His Command Series:**

Controlling Her Pleasure

Commanding Her Trust

Claiming Her Heart

**The Bought by the Billionaire Series:**

Dark Domination

Deep Domination

Desperate Domination

Divine Domination

**The Kidnapped by the Billionaire Series:**

Dirty Twisted Love

Filthy Wicked Love

Crazy Beautiful Love

One More Shameless Night

**The Bedding the Bad Boy Series:**

The Bad Boy's Temptation

The Bad Boy's Seduction

The Bad Boy's Redemption

Printed in Great Britain
by Amazon